Relapse

A Novel

SRIKANT VERMA

Translated by Krishna Baldev Vaid

SPEAKING TIGER

SPEAKING TIGER PUBLISHING PVT LTD
4381/4 Ansari Road, Daryaganj,
New Delhi–110002, India

First published in English translation by
Vikas Publishing House 1975
This edition published by Speaking Tiger in paperback 2018

ISBN: 978-93-88070-56-0
e-ISBN: 978-93-88070-57-7

10 9 8 7 6 5 4 3 2 1

Typeset in Charter BT by Jojy Philip
Printed at Sanat Printers, Kundli

Srikant Verma was a novelist, short-story writer, journalist and literary critic, but he is best known as one of the most significant figures of the Naya Kavita movement in modern Hindi poetry. Written in the realist mode, his poems are marked by anger, dissent and protest, and hold up an urgent mirror to the evils in society. His most famous poetic work is *Magadh*, for which he received the Sahitya Akademi Award. Other works include the poetry collections *Bhatka Megh*, *Maya Darpan* and *Jalsaghar*; collections of short stories *Jhadi* and *Samvad*; a travelogue *Apollo Ka Rath*; and a book of interviews, *Beeswin Sadi Ke Andhere Mein*. A part of the Indian National Congress, he was also a Member of Parliament for almost a decade. Srikant Verma died in 1986.

Krishna Baldev Vaid is a noted Hindi playwright, novelist and short-story writer. He is also an academic who taught English at various Indian and American universities before retiring from the State University of New York. A prolific writer, his books include the novels *Uska Bachpan*, *Ek Naukrani Ki Diary, Guzara Hua Zamana* and *Nar Nari*; the plays *Mona Lisa Ki Muskaan*, *Bhookh Aag Hai* and *Pariwar Akhada*; and the short-story collections *Mera Dushman*, *Bodhisatva Ki Biwi* and *Pita Ki Parchhaiyan*. His work has been translated into Japanese, Polish, German, Russian, Italian as well as several Indian languages.

1

An inland letter lay on the table. I picked it up. It was her handwriting. I was surprised as well as intrigued. It was a brief note asking me to see her.

If two persons sit down across a table with a grim vow to wear each other out in a contest of silence, and one of them should finally break down after a long and painful period of stubborn unfriendliness, the other is bound to feel more confident of himself. That note from Bindo after several years of silence produced in me a similar feeling. But there was an important difference; we were no longer sitting across the same table; I had got up and gone over to another.

I got dressed hurriedly and went up to the roof. The sky was sunny and clear. A glider circled merrily above my head. The day seemed good to me. After many days. Again.

It was winter and the time about eleven. That was the hour she had suggested. But I didn't plan to be on time. This is one of my recently adopted strategems. One should never be on time to meet a woman, for it amounts to accepting that moment, if not that woman, as one's destiny. In the past I had suffered an unnecessary lot because of this addiction to punctuality.

So I decided to walk part of the way in order to be late. That, I thought, would be my punishment, not for myself but for her. If I was late by a half hour or so, she'd give me an angry and disappointed look, which would be my reward and I'd feel pleased with myself.

As I approached her place, I had a brief feeling of unreality. Also a passing thought that I was making a mistake. I felt I was about to open an old diary without the necessary self-assurance to face what I had scribbled there so long ago. But hadn't that diary already become a mere museum piece? The writing there would hardly make any difference, would it? I was determined to turn its pages with detachment.

Soon enough I realized I'd been all wrong. There was no angry disappointment on her face. Only an impenetrable hardness. Instead of getting up to greet me or asking me to sit down she gave me one look and kept sitting there. For a moment I felt inwardly pleased. After all those years she was still clinging to the old understanding that I didn't have to be treated formally. But the very next moment I was furious at her presumptuousness.

Acting like a stranger, I asked her permission to sit down and she looked at me with contempt and some pain. But apparently she knew I'd be cold and formal.

She pushed a chair toward me. I started scanning the room and things in an effort to evade her eyes. Nothing had changed except that she struck me as being very lonesome.

I was a bit taken aback to see my picture on the shelf. But I didn't let her on. The picture faced her. She must have done that deliberately. I tried to steal a glance at her. Her eyes were empty. I felt some pity for her but I averted my eyes and started looking at that shelf.

Coming upon one's old picture after several years is an unsettling experience. Especially when the picture is soaked in intimate associations. One is fond of the picture and wants to believe one is still the same person.

I had had that picture taken at Bindo's insistence. Whenever I used to be in that room I was always aware of that picture as our witness who kept a close eye on everything I did. I knew that after her morning bath when Bindo burnt incense in the room she always put two sticks near my picture.

"You are a backward Hindu girl, Bindo! Look at you worshipping this stupid picture. Why not worship me!"

"I do not worship anything. All I do is to try to purify my unfortunately impure possessions!"

If that picture of mine on the shelf were to turn around and look at me, it is sure to be surprised by our dissimilarity and, I believe, it will be disgusted with me.

Bindo had her empty eyes fixed on the outside and I realized we had little to say to each other. I shouldn't have come.

Perhaps she sensed my constraint intuitively. When the servant brought tea she asked him to put our chairs out on the lawn.

Outside it was sunny and warm. I felt a bit revived. The day began to look fresh and good again.

I watched her hands as she poured tea. Her fingers seemed to have changed colour. Her green pullover looked lovely against the lawn.

She handed me the cup and put three

spoonfuls of sugar in it. She remembers my taste in sugar.

After about ten minutes of tea I began to feel bored. If that was all, and she knew it was, why in hell had she asked me over?

I gave her an abrupt glance and saw she had been watching me. She didn't take her eyes off me as she sipped her tea.

Well, why can't I make the first move? There's no point in blaming it all on her. After all nothing more than little talk is possible between the two of us.

She was making me a second cup of tea. I knew she does everything with complete concentration. While pouring a cup of tea she seems to be pouring herself out. This is the best time to start. She won't consider it unnatural.

"Where have you been?" I asked in a low voice.

She stopped short as if her ears had been awaiting my question. She looked askance at me. Are you trying to dupe me again! Then she wiped her face with the apron of her sari as she said, "Poona, Panchmarhi, Amritsar."

"A strange combination! North, west, centre! How come?"

"Research."

"I thought you'd given that up?"

"Since I had nothing else to do I decided to resume an old preoccupation."

"Not at your age!" I could've bitten my tongue. One's discrimination is always at the mercy of one's stupid tongue. I really regretted my remark. But she seemed neither shocked nor offended.

I've always felt small compared to Bindo. But I've never completely accepted that I am. Very few men know that women like men precisely for what they themselves take to be their smallness. Perhaps it is because women think that small men are essentially naive and incapable of dissimulation.

I tried to look serious and prim.

"Would you like to go out for lunch?"

"Anywhere you like."

This "anywhere" was familiar to me. It meant she was completely at my disposal for the occasion. I was a bit alarmed at this. I had strayed from Bindo's street into another bylane. Going back to where she stood would mean once again a loss of my bearings.

She came back from the other room with another sari on and started straightening her dry loose hairbun. I looked at her with desire. I knew her kind of beauty was rare. Her chiseled figure, her elusive complexion, her sharpness! Years ago I'd felt proud of my ability to disengage myself from a woman as beautiful as Bindo. As I looked at her standing on the green lawn in glorious sunshine I felt a keen desire for her and a sweet sensation at the thought that for years her ravishing body had been mine and that I'd seen it naked.

I felt rather awkward walking on the street beside her. I couldn't determine the distance I should keep between myself and her. Distance is always a problem while walking beside somebody with whom your relationship is not quite clear. But for this I wouldn't have stopped a taxi and felt a great relief when it did stop. I opened the door for her but she didn't step in. I'd forgotten that she always insisted on my entering first so that she could sit on my left. But as I refused to follow our old practice I saw a quick flash of anger in her eyes which she suppressed in the next instant.

I had walked those streets with Bindo in that mood so many times that by now they had all gone dead for me. But it was the first time for me to find them odd and to feel as if I had been locked up in a taxi with my antagonist.

I could see her face in the mirror in front of me. She seemed to have recovered her composure. In fact she looked so normal and at case that I was irritated. During the years of our separation I had examined her afresh and arrived at an altogether new image of her.

The same exchanges, incidents and gestures had a different meaning now and I came to the conclusion that Bindo was a conceited woman and every action of hers was motivated by her desire to prove that I was inferior to her in every respect. Her restraint too was hypocritical which compelled me to feel that there was no stability in my character, that it was riddled with holes and that as long as I had this flaw she considered me unworthy of her. And it was great of her that she stooped down to me. This realization aroused a rebellion against Bindo, in my mind, that was retaliatory and vengefully violent. But in the final analysis I found myself helpless. Her composed reflection in the taxi mirror gave rise to such fury in me that to distract myself I started looking at the buildings outside.

The taxi driver tried to dodge an oncoming truck, and Bindo's body nearly fell on me. If this had happened a few years earlier, I would have pulled her over to me but nothing happened this time. A little later when I looked in the mirror and found her face drawn and fallen as if her expression had been disintegrated by the taxi's single swerve. I am not used to this expression on her face and I lowered my eyes in in indecision and shame and agony. We seemed suddenly separated by a mournful sadness.

When the taxi stopped, she got down and I felt she and I were visiting the tomb of our dead child.

The presence of a child brings about a wonderful intimacy between incomplete men and women, the like of which is not brought about by conversations, vows, kisses, and quarrels but a dead child does not bind a man and a woman, it separates them silently and secretly as they hold each other responsible for his untimely death.

I had brought her again to a simple but good old restaurant. We never went to posh restaurants like the middle class couples and families who eat there in fear and insecurity as if they are on a banquet uninvited and haunted by the fear that they may be asked to show their invitation card any moment.

Our usual table in that restaurant was, by a lucky chance, unoccupied even that day. In fact, the entire restaurant had a deserted look except for a few girls and boys who were there at a couple of tables eating in noisy, familiar informality. Among the waiters there were several old faces but even they had completely forgotten us. They scanned us carefully as if they were trying to guess the tip we'd leave them.

One waiter saluted us and placed the menu on the table. After I had pushed the menu to Bindo and realized that I'd committed a mistake. During our final days together, I began to think that my gravest mistake was that I had given the decision-making authority in almost every matter to Bindo. But my realization was too late because in our final days together when I had tried to take back some decision-making rights, I found that Bindo resented this and our relationship began to crack. But today I noticed that Bindo was indifferent. Her expression went through a number of changes before she realized that I was waiting for her to give the order. "What will 'aap' have?" she asked me formally. The formal "aap" she had used for me gave me a jolt. But when I looked at her, she repeated the question using "aap" again.

She beckoned the waiter and placed the order with deliberate slowness.

After the waiter had placed all the dishes at the table, I noticed that all my favourite dishes were there. I told the waiter to take back the chicken dish. After the water had gone she asked me "Why?"

"I've been having digestion problems."

She knew it was a lie. Of all the things before me I liked the chicken dish best and would have even if my stomach had been truly upset.

"Since when?"

I scanned her face. Was she being sarcastic? I felt like telling her that since her departure but there she was taking a bite off the bread. It bugs me, partly I guess because of envy, the way women get absorbed in eating no matter what the circumstances are.

I tried to contain my anger as I answered, "For the last few days."

"Have you been to a doctor?" she asked as she took another morsel.

"Yes, of course!" My irritation was mounting.

"What did he say?"

I thought I'd explode and say something silly. But I was determined not to explode, not to lose my cool, not ever to cry again in front of a woman. These were the lessons I had learnt from her.

"Nothing much." I said in a calm tone and began to eat so as to cut the conversation off.

What does she want? Obviously, she wants something or she wouldn't be here. I hadn't turned her out; she had left on her own. In fact I had cried over her going. And it was I who had tried to woo her back. So why is she here now? Is it in order to see with her woman's eyes how I am managing without her? Idiot!

She had finished eating and started staring at me.

When I asked the waiter to bring the bill she interrupted me and ordered coffee.

She made a cup of coffee for me. That bunch of boys and girls had left. As long as they were there I had an excuse for looking away from her. Now that we were alone in the restaurant I began to feel nervous. There are times when you need noise, inferior music, and crowds. Had there been a jukebox around I might have managed to cope with my awkwardness.

Whenever I eat a little late in the afternoon I get a headache. As we came out I had a heavy head. A flower boy started following us, "Flowers for the lady!"

She took some money out of her purse and bought a bracelet. In old days I often bought her one and gallantly tied it either round her hair or her wrist. I used to think with pleasure of the people looking enviously at me. Even later when things had started going wrong, whenever she bought a bracelet I would tie it for her and in our worst crises her face would become rapturous.

I had walked her to the taxi stand but was at a loss for words of farewell. After she sat got a taxi and I was about to walk away without saying a word, she asked, “Look, can’t you stay with me awhile more?”

I felt like saying a curt “No” but on looking into her eyes I saw she really wanted me to stay.

“Where shall we go?” I asked as I sat beside her.

“Wherever you like!”

If she really meant that why had she left me?

“To Qutub,” I told the driver without a thought.

She kept winding that bracelet of flowers round her wrist and fondling it.

I wanted to know what she had to say. After several years, she had come back on her own and taken her stand in the court, so to speak, without any warrant from me. In fact there wasn’t any court until she had come. She had brought it along with her.

During November and December Qutub is crowded but I have been there in April and May too when there is hardly anybody around and the whole world looks like a waste land as hot wind comes to you from the ruins and deserted bushes around you. And when your awareness of your existence is more personal. As I used to lie beside Bindo in the bushes I often thought that if someone happened to stray that way he would stop short and think that a male panther had just finished with a female panther and was now lying next to her in complete exhaustion.

There was a crowd of picnickers. I avoided them and walked over to a patch of grass away from them. Young girls and boys were taking pictures of one another with Qutub in the background. A guide was going on and on to a group of foreign tourists. And a few women were throwing orange peels around on the grass as they ate oranges.

Bindo followed me to where I sat. She took off her pullover and started straightening her sari that kept slipping off her shoulder again and again.

"Would you like a cup of tea?" she asked, pointing to the restaurant in front of us.

"No, I have a headache."

"Oh!" she said and fell silent. Then she looked toward the group of people next to us, looked at her watch, and asked, "What time is it by your watch?"

"Fifteen past five."

"Oh! Mine is a bit fast."

For some time there was silence between us. Then she said, "Shall we leave?"

But even after I got up she kept sitting. She looked at me a moment, picked up her pullover, got up and was ready to go. Her walk was quick. Then she said as we walked, "I wanted to talk to you about something."

Talk! What else did we do but talk for years! What is left now to talk about! I was furious, as I turned these words over in my mind. But all I actually said was, "Well, I am here."

"Forget it." She picked up her pace.

Vain woman! I was so irritated and could hardly wait until I could hop into a cab or something and get away from her. A little further we got a cab. I got in and stretched myself as if she wasn't with me. She got in and sat down apart from me. For the first time I felt I wasn't inferior to her. When the taxi stopped at her place she got out and said, "Look, I want to offer you an apology."

I was attentive. At the mention of apology I felt a little pity for her. And before it even overflowed, she had seen through me.

“I am sorry that I put you to so much trouble today,” she said and walked away. I was taken aback. Then I stabilized myself slowly and looked out the window, trying to see whether she was going away irritated or defeated. I saw nothing but simple retreat in her walk.

On returning to my place I turned the light on and told the servant not to cook for me as I didn’t feel too well. Then I changed and turned off the light and lay down on my bed. Under my third-floor flat there was an orchestra of various sounds—horns, human noises, words. Stretched between the darkness inside and the noise out I was very restless and that restlessness could be quenched only by a woman’s body; it was quite easy for me to get myself a woman’s body; it had always been easy, but the fear of giving myself up was greater than my desire.

2

My eyes were irritated when I got up rather late in the morning. I looked out the window, sourly, and closed my eyes again. My head was heavy. My body under the quilt was unquiet. I pushed the quilt to the foot of the bed, lay down prone, my head pressed to the pillow, trying hard to go back to sleep. But instead, the events of the day past came rushing back to me.

I have been through this torment a number of times and know what hell is like.

Ah well! The first thing to do is to get rid of this headache. I asked my servant to bring me two tablets.

"Anacin or Aspro?"

"Whatever there is!"

I got up and put my head under the tap. Cold water passed through my hair and on to my neck and back. It cooled my body as well as mind.

Thanks to the water and to the tablets, not to speak of will power, I began to feel quite active and keen for the sun. I decided to go out for a cup of coffee. "But where? Anywhere?" Reminded of her through this fragment of her sentence I was startled.

I straightened my tie as I walked, self-absorbed, on a street lined by stores and teashops. After I had left all those little shops behind I stopped and began to wait for a taxi. At some distance from me there was a bus-stop and a long line of bus awaiters. The street was a flowing stream of cyclists. The morning in this neighbourhood comes with the curse of office workers and evening with the doom of domesticity. The deadness of the evening is matched only by the misery of the morning.

On reaching Connaught Place I entered the familiar twilight of a restaurant I liked. That twilight was friendly and cooperative, bringing people together when they wanted to or keeping them apart, if they so desired.

There were several clusters of fashionable girls and boys at various tables talking in near whispers. At a table in a corner there were three acquaintances of mine who invited me to join them. When I didn't respond, one of them, a fellow whom I had known for the shortest time, got up and came over to me, "Are you waiting for someone?"

I peered into his eyes for any innuendo but there wasn't any. "No," I said. I was wondering what I should do with him, offer him a coffee or what, when he got up and went back to his table. I felt relieved and reclined against the wall. When the waiter came for my order I asked for coffee and resumed my posture and closed my eyes. The odour and laughter of the people around began gradually to seep into my body and for the first time I felt it was a new day. Then I opened my eyes suddenly. Suppose someone is watching me! The thought of being watched was like a thorn. But I saw that everybody was absorbed in their own activities.

At a table in front of me sat four girls whose every gesture proclaimed they were four girls. Closer still sat a couple amorously close to each other, lost to all but each other. At a table to my right sat a foreigner and an Indian eating a heavy breakfast. In front of me sat my coffee which I found had gone cold. I poured that cold coffee into my cup and sipped it with great relish. After a few sips I felt stable and self-assured at the thought that I wasn't a stranger to that place, that I was part of that family, even though I had come back there after a long time.

Does she still come to this place? The sight of the waiter silently waiting for another order bothered me. The front door opened and brought in a rustling of saris and a clink of bracelets.

"I don't need anything else."

But the waiter hadn't heard me.

"Look, bring me my bill."

The waiter walked away for the bill. I was annoyed. As if someone had broken the glass pane of my window. I stared at the waiter as he came back with the bill and felt even more irritated.

"Wait, get me another coffee."

The waiter went away for another coffee.

The old crowd had been replaced by a new crowd. The place looked livelier but the presence of so many people was not pleasant. Almost all of them were unknown to me. Even during the days I used to come there often the place was always busy at about that time but I knew almost everyone there. It was quite a different world now.

I was just about to relax after my second coffee when a whole bunch of people came and took their stand near my table waiting for me to get up. Such scenes are quite common. Four people silently demanding that a solitary sitter yield his table to them while that man sits and chews his cud oblivious of their existence.

On coming out into the light I found everything back in its groove. I had nothing to do but walk around aimlessly. After I had taken one round of Connaught Place the question came up—where now?

Janpath at this time is quite colourful thanks to women who have nothing to do except shopping. And there are young girls lolling from one shop to another, their packages pressed to their bosoms of various sizes, drinking Coca Cola every now and again.

Strolling along Janpath I stopped at a shop festooned with a colourful variety of saris to attract customers. I had an impulse to touch them once.

"Please step in," said the shopkeeper, and I crushed my silly impulse and walked on.

As I retraced my steps from the other end of the row of shops on Janpath I felt even worse. Everybody else is eating, drinking, enjoying himself in the company of friends, reading, and in this whole city I am the only one wasting my time on nothing. I had come out of my place to enjoy myself and it was only two in the afternoon and there was a whole lot of day and night still to go through.

The thought of going home was horrifying. I toyed with the idea of spending some time in the library until the idea died. It wasn't the first time I had felt like that. The same thing had happened before, many times. But in the meanwhile the rest of the world had gone beyond getting and eating. The train had deserted the platform so long ago that it was hard to revive the awareness of that train having ever stopped there.

Once again caught in the circle of Connaught Place I found myself standing in front of the place where the previous day Bindo and I had had lunch. My heart missed a beat. I put my hand in my pocket and took out that letter after and because of which the whole affair had started again.

I opened the letter and looked at it again and noticed an affectation in the writing. As I stepped off the curb I tore that letter into pieces and threw them up in air. I wished that those pieces would fly all the way to her apartment and fall on her face. That mean woman!

I crossed the street and entered the park

generally inhabited by poor peons and coolies or by idlers. I chose a spot in the corner and spread my handkerchief on the grass. After a while I took off my jacket, lay down, and covered my head with the jacket. This was much better than any other activity.

After the sun had slid off my body I began to feel cold. The same old horrible darkness was descending. I got up and returned to the crowds of Connaught Place, muttering to myself, "I'll never get out of this labryinth." Just then a foreign couple brushed past me with great aplomb.

What is it that she wants after all! As the twilight increased, my irritation grew. I'll have to take a decision. But then as I got into the taxi I asked myself if I hadn't already taken that decision after all.

When the taxi stopped at her place I noticed that her room was lit. I had caught her at the right time. All I wanted to ask her was why she had come. I entered their front lawn and suddenly realized that I was acting like a crazy fellow. What was the point of visiting her? Won't she be delighted to see me the way I didn't want her to be? Won't she be radiant with triumph?

I turned and walked out of the yard. I could

see her through the window. She was busy knitting as usual and her face was calm. What a fraud! I hurried away, thinking that with time everything would resolve itself and peace would return.

I decided to go some place for a bite and then return home to some book. When I reached home after a long walk it was late night. The servant looked sulky. I hadn't told him whether I would be home for dinner or not. Possibly he hadn't cooked even for himself but I wasn't going to let that bother me. The sight of Bindo's calm had given me back my calm and I had decided that the entire tension was futile, that I was fine all by myself.

I took some money out of my pocket and asked the servant to go out and get himself a meal. He left but was back in a moment. "There was a call for you."

"Who was it?"

"Whoever it was didn't give me any name."

I went through the list of possible callers but couldn't think of a likely candidate. Then suddenly I thought of her with a start and asked, "Was it a man or a woman!"

"A lady."

"Oh!" And as he was going out I asked, "Did

she leave a message? Did she say she'd call again?"

"She said nothing."

I knew it was Bindo. The fact that she had phoned me gave me pleasure and I began to whistle.

It was impossible that she wouldn't call again. Knowing her was knowing her forever. But what has she to say to me? The thought that she might apologize gave me even greater joy.

Normally, I'd have gone to sleep but I got up and lit the stove and put on the kettle for coffee. After years I enjoyed making coffee for myself. It was good coffee too. It was ten now. Waiting for Bindo's phone call was getting to be as painful as the long wait through the summer vacation for the final exam results used to be.

I was sure that unless I was all wrong about Bindo she would call again. But it was getting on to be eleven. I got up and started pacing the floor. Outside it was all quiet. A policeman leaned against the electric pole with his coat collars turned up. But if it wasn't her phone who else could it be? And why had she called? I recalled the calm of her face and decided it was false.

I brought the phone close to my bed and

dialled her number like a blind man. I knew she'd pick it up. When she did so I asked her a straight question, "Was it you who called me?"

"No," she answered tersely.

I felt as if she had pushed me over the bed. I got up, brushed my pants, and shouted, "You are a liar!"

"I beg your pardon!"

I heard a note of astonishment in her voice. I know that if I had shouted at her like that in the old days she would have curled her lips and rejoined, "That becomes you!" And after that she'd have put the receiver down. But this time her tone seemed to suggest as if someone had got a wrong number.

My fingers around the receiver were trembling. I said in a quivering voice, "What is it that you want after all?" And I felt as if after that question I had suddenly grown old and weary. From the other end there was neither an answer not the sound of the receiver being put down.

"Why don't you answer me? What is it that you want?" As compared to my voice there was far more fury in my veins but I couldn't have possibly expressed that.

"Anything more?" she asked expressionlessly.

I felt I had been floored once again. This time I didn't have the heart to get up.

"Is there anything more you want to say?" she repeated in the same tone.

I hung up, and taking off my shoes and clothes, flung them around. I felt as if I had been bayonetted and all I could do was to blurt out curses and swear words. Mean! Cheat! Liar! Faithless!

Normally after one has hurled abuses like that at a woman one feels ashamed. But I felt nothing of the sort because it was Bindo I had abused.

After I had become a little unburdened I realized that the abuses I had uttered were the ones normally reserved for one's own woman.

3

This is the story of my miserable days. I am not sure whether those days were quite as miserable for Bindo.

Now that it is all over I have come to the conclusion that inwardly I am unclear and unstable. Outwardly I am otherwise thanks to my many masks. And those who don't see through the masks have a different impression about me. They are quite capable of being overawed and even overwhelmed by me.

But Bindo knows me inside out. She knew how to manipulate me. I have devoted a lot of attention to myself, and she has never perhaps thought as much about me. But she knows me more than I know myself.

The thought that someone knows me like that frightens me, I can't forget the time when after Bindo and I broke apart this fear became a part of my being. Just before leaving me she had said, “I can quite understand why you fall on your knees before me. Had I not known you you’d have been a different man altogether.”

Thousands of words have been exchanged between the two of us but I’ll never forget this observation of hers and am prepared to forgive her numerous falsehoods for the sake of the one great truth she uttered when she said that.

No game is more dangerous than disrobing oneself to the point when there is nothing between you and the others. That is what I did right at the outset. I was in a great hurry to fling aside all my coverings in front of her. The game finished no sooner than it started. One feels ashamed of one’s nakedness when one is alone. My shame also started after Bindo left me. It was shame with a touch of anger. It was only after she had left that I realized that it was she who had exposed me.

It was my second sleepless night. When finally I did doze off towards early morning I was out till late in the day. On waking up I found myself surrounded by the familiar objects in my room except for one little spot inside me that was full of emptiness. Sleep had perhaps relaxed my head without lightening my heart.

There was a time when I used to feel light after giving vent to my disgust but something had changed within me it seemed. The disgust I thought I had spilled out was back.

The floor was littered with butt ends that I had thrown around in hate and anger. My own room looked ominous and menacing.

The servant was busy dusting up the place. But he was abnormally quiet and cautious. Perhaps he knew. I looked at him and found he was absorbed in his servitude. His greatest problem just then was dust.

Every morning the newspaper boy delivers several newspapers. The first thing I do in the morning is to go through those papers, one after the other. This takes me through two or three hours every morning. The last two days' papers however lay in a heap, untouched. There was a roll of dirty clothes in one corner. The bed sheets were all rumpled. I looked at everything in the room and it looked disorderly and wrong. I myself was wrong. Sometimes an awareness of being wrong is reassuring. But I wasn't in a position to decide whether my greatest need at that time was reassurance or something else.

As I came out of my apartment, scrubbed and clean, I resolved not to let things drift along.

When one is sick one goes to a doctor of some sort. But when one is sick as well as not sick, like me, what can one do? I was prepared to pay whatever price was necessary to get out of all that mess.

There is a man who knows all about my problems. I didn't want him to be my witness but there he was. It wasn't my fault. Bindo herself had told him everything just before she had left. Not that he had no inkling on his own. Most probably he had. Perhaps he knew exactly the way it had been. The beginning as well as the end. And all the twists and turns in between. But he had never shown any interest in listening to an explanation from either of us. Perhaps Bindo and I had been attracted to him because of his reserve. But both of us knew very well that none other than he knew all the intricacies and nuances of our relationship. All the same I had never taken Anil into confidence about the complications of this years-old affair.

It is quite a coincidence that just as I was about to burst before him she did. Had she delayed even for a few more days I'd have put everything before Anil. The time had come for that. And perhaps I had no other alternative than making someone privy to all my pain before breaking with Bindo. But Bindo, who never acts rashly, had saved me this once by her rashness.

Even now it seems to me that had Bindo not told Anil and Anil in his turn not told me that Bindo did, our relationship would not have come to such an absolute end. But of course she had told him with full consciousness of the consequences. Perhaps she wanted to wash her hands off everything by telling him. With her disclosure she had raised her own prestige. She had told him that she couldn't carry on with me any more and that he should inform me accordingly. Now I understand why she conveyed this message to me through Anil. If she had wanted to there was nothing to stop her from coming straight to me and telling me to my face. She had never been afraid of me, had no reason to be so either.

But she wanted to remain firm. She might have thought that my misery would break her resolve. It would be hard for anyone to believe that a man can actually fall at a woman's feet. But the fear of estrangement and of loneliness had forced me to fall at her feet so many times during our relationship. In fact, had I not done so she wouldn't have left me. After numerous prostrations I had raised her so high that during the last days she must have begun to regard me as a shackle round her feet.

It is all the more odd that every time I fell at her feet I not only raised her but thought I had raised myself too. I used to think that my strength lay in my ability to lie low before her.

She saw through this so-called strength of mine. Before I could even plead with her she broke apart abruptly and then by justifying herself before a third person she had turned our separation into an accomplished fact.

When I reached Anil's place he was warming himself at the heater, ready to leave. It was colder than usual. There was mist and the sky was unclear. It looked like rain. I had been quite hesitant about going to see Anil after so many months. In fact as soon as I stepped in I had a desire to turn around and leave. But then I somehow mustered enough strength to persist. Anil turned to me and smiled.

"Are you going to work?" It was a stupid question.

"Aren't you?"

"Can you be absent for today?"

"What's the matter?" he got up and moved his chair toward me.

He was examining me. My clothes were clean,

my hair was brushed, my shoes were shining and my tie was trim. He was quite unkempt compared to me. In fact, with his pullover and dhoti and socks and slippers, it seemed as if he hadn't even washed himself.

"Sit down and relax."

He was looking at me with great curiosity. Normally, I feel revolted by others' curiosity about me. People are always fond of peeping through keyholes and some of them don't hesitate to peer even into others' windows while walking by. They seem to think they should not miss the fun or the theatre that is perhaps going on in there.

Anil is different. He has never bothered to know what goes on in someone's house. He doesn't pry. The greatest basis, perhaps the one basis, of our friendship was that unless I let him he wouldn't take the initiative in anything.

Nothing irritates me more than someone pushing me. Every time it was Bindo who had coerced me into exposing myself. I was always afraid that her pressure would break my back and disintegrate me. I used to feel at the slightest pressure that there she was curbing my freedom. Anil, on the contrary, was always a great relief. There was no insistence or demand on his part. His ease used to put me at ease too.

"I have some important matter to discuss with you," I said and looked at him apprehensively.

"Let's have tea first," he said with great ease.

Anil's room always made me feel that living properly is not the prerogative of married people. I should have learnt from Anil the art of living decently—without tension and extravagance.

"Well, if it's just a matter of a little talk, I'll go to the office a bit late."

What I really wanted to ask him was to see if he could spend the whole day with me.

"It looks like rain and if it does rain it will get colder. And it will be all the more difficult for the poor." Anil seemed to be talking to himself.

"That's true," I said without much interest.

"It is the poor who really suffer in every season—the heat in summer, the rain in the rainy season, the cold in winter."

I kept quiet.

"The climate of our country! Half of one's life is wasted in fighting the weather. That is why we can't accomplish much."

I felt a bit irritated by his obsession with weather. But I have to put up with his whims, I told myself cunningly, for after all why should

I expect him to bother about my problems? He has no reason to be very keen. Besides it is not his nature to be too keen about anything. Had he been in my place he would have kept his cool. A woman is not a whole universe to him but just a figure out of many on the landscape of this universe. His character is different from mine, a fact for which neither he nor I am to blame.

"How much sugar?" he asked, his eyes fixed on mine.

Is he trying to size me up?

"Two spoonfuls," I said nervously, and in order to avoid some other indiscretion, repeated with a view to getting a hold on myself, "Look, I want to talk to you about something."

"I know," he said as he took a sip of this tea. "The weather is so bad that I like even my own tea."

He was being evasive. Did he take me for an idiot? He was relishing his tea. With every sip he seemed to be saying, "Look at me, this is how one should relish tea, you don't know how to; look at me!"

I felt another wave of irritation at him. It was impossible that a person of his insight should not have noticed my anxiety. Then why is he behaving like this? Is he trying to ignore me? Is he putting me off? Years ago he had said once: "When you are really getting impatient to say something, put a lump of sugar on your tongue and see if your tongue doesn't prefer that lump to talking." Maybe he was signalling me to keep quiet.

He must be mistaken. Surely he thinks I have come to pick his brain about impersonal matters and that I'll bore him with my intellectual outpourings. After all my monologues he used to say, "Every question is its own question and nobody can do much about it." With this remark he used to dispel all my precious piffle.

"Look, I am not here today for our usual chat."

"So you've come to talk about your marriage?" he asked with a smile.

"I am in no mood for frivolity at this moment," I said.

I thought he'd see that I was serious and would become so himself.

"Who is being frivolous?" he said pouring tea for himself. "How about another cup?"

"No."

"Come on, have another, it'll warm you up a bit more."

I kept quiet. Anil is quite impressive to look

at. He looks even more impressive in a dhoti. As I sat there looking at his impressive figure, I didn't know where to start.

"It seems this weather has made you more irritable," he said.

"The weather has had a worse effect on you. You have no time for anyone else," I said with genuine anger. "I've been sitting here for almost an hour listening to your babble about weather and tea."

"What else is there to talk about?" He knew how to ward off an attack with one sentence. That is why he was happy.

Now he was collecting dirty dishes with the dexterity of a housewife. He should have been a woman.

"It is drizzling already," he cried.

I saw it was.

"I told you it would rain." He was jubilant at the truth or his prediction.

Now I was really angrier with him than at Bindo. He was playing with me. He knew I was unhappy and that made him happy. It seems one man's low is another man's high.

He saw through my agitation. After putting the dishes away properly he came and sat down next to me. Both of us lit our cigarettes.

"What have you been doing all these days?" he said as he came closer.

"Doing? I've been roasting in hell."

"Where?"

"Right here."

"I was under the impression you'd gone out."

"What made you think so?"

"Oh, I don't know."

"Have you given up the idea of marriage?" he asked with unabated ease.

"Yes."

"I'd hoped you'd reconsider your decision."

"You should have been the last person to hope that."

At my sharp retort he smiled faintly. Then he did a very mean thing. He curled this lips and blew out a ring of smoke. The ring rose a little, then grew thin until it dissolved. Then he put his cigarette out, drew himself a bit closer and said, "Was it something special you wanted to talk about?"

"No," I said irritably.

He smiled sarcastically and said, "No matter. If you have nothing to say, I have. Do you know?"

"What?"

Seeing that I was interested his eyes lit up. "Do you know that Bindo is here?"

I almost jumped out of my seat. On seeing me so excited he looked pleased and he leaned back.

"You do know then?"

"How do you know?"

"Has she been to see you?" I made another raid on his silence.

"No!" he said rather harshly. "But I have seen her."

"Where?"

"Near Regal."

There are several shops and a couple of restaurants near Regal that she likes. But she never visited those places alone. Always with me. She used to say she was afraid of crossing that street alone. "I am scared of crossing this street; I keep imagining I'll die crossing this narrow street; I'll be run over by something!"

"Was she with someone?"

He saw through my panic and tried to drown it by saying, "Even if she was how does it matter to you?"

"Who was she with?"

"She was alone. But why are you getting so hot under the collar?"

I kept quiet. And he went on, "What difference does it make to you? I am amazed at your anxiety."

As I looked away I thought Anil had changed a lot. Previously he couldn't stand seeing me self-exposed. It used to terrify him. Now he was probing me, prying into me. I felt revolted. It was raining. The window panes were covered with mist. It was miserable weather. And for the first time Anil's company was becoming unbearable.

"How about a cup of coffee?" he said and broke the silence between us.

I kept quiet.

"This rain threatens to go on and on. That is the worst part of rain in winter. I always depresses me. I don't feel like going to work and staying in doesn't seem any better. What time is it anyway? How will I get to my office?"

I felt Anil was a coward. And commonplace. Office, apartment, and himself! That was his entire world. So small. Perhaps he had narrowed it recently. Previously it wasn't so. But there was no shadow on his face. Perhaps all he wanted was to make me realize I was wasting his time.

When I got up to leave, he said, "But how can you go out in this rain?"

"I'll manage."

"Wait for it to stop." As I stepped out, he said, "You won't be able to see her at this time even if you want to." This was mean. I noticed his face had become very coarse. On other occasions he was quite capable of unwinding and becoming relaxed. But now he was confronting me. "I know everything," he said without getting up.

"What is that?"

"That she has been to see you."

I wasn't startled at his reply. I knew he was sounding me out, that he was guessing. I felt like saying, "You are stupid."

"I can see it on your face that you have had a quarrel with her."

He looked surprised at my silence. Perhaps he was wondering at the source of my strength.

As I came out on the street in the rain I thought I had come to Anil for advice but actually I had taught him a lesson. As I was coming out he had shouted, "Wait for me!" But I hadn't waited for him.

It wasn't a new thing for me to run after a taxi in the rain. I had done that on innumerable occasions in cold and in rain while she waited inside a store or under some other protection. And after getting into one I would wipe my head and face with my handkerchief like a "hero".

But that day while I was getting soaked in the rain I didn't feel like a hero but an idiot.

Why hadn't I waited for a few minutes? What was my hurry? Why the hell did I run out of Anil's place? Finally as I got into a taxi at the taxi stand I realized that I had harmed myself more than Anil. I asked the driver to take me to Regal. My clothes were wet but I couldn't think of going back home. The rain was slowing down.

Because of rain the streets were deserted. So probably were restaurants. I stood outside one waiting for the rain to stop. The rain didn't really bother me much. It could go on for the rest of the day for all I cared.

"Near Regal!"

"Was she with someone?"

"How does it matter to you even if she was!"

This exchange between Anil and me was still bothering me. She must have been with someone. She is not used to going out alone. She is fond of company because she is never the one to get hurt by companionship. Cohabitation with her is oppressive not for her but for the other party. She runs away from loneliness, never from company. She wasn't being frivolous when she said that she was scared of crossing the street by herself.

Perhaps it was her loneliness that first

attracted me. Had she been social like other girls I wouldn't have been drawn to her. I had realized in the very beginning that it would be difficult to penetrate her loneliness and possess her.

That was a very familiar spot for both of us. Whenever she was happy she stopped abruptly while passing by that place. I would understand that she wanted a betel leaf. I would order a soft leaf for her and offer it to her when it was ready. She would frown faintly, which told me that I had again forgotten to have the leaf scented. And after I'd repaired my mistake and returned I'd find she had already moved on.

Now the rain had stopped completely. People had started coming out on streets. Along the edges and even in the middle of some streets a great deal of rain water was flowing fast. There were stray clouds still in the sky. And it had grown much colder. All my clothes including the jacket were soaking wet, sticking to my body. I could feel the cold deep under my skin.

There are a few small shops on Irwin Road where even now I go in my lonesome moments. In those places I don't feel like a stranger because I never run into any familiar face over there. Those places are visited only by the poorest of the poor for they are extremely inexpensive. As I made my way through several rivulets of water to a small tea shop I felt relieved. Tea was served in a glass and as I sipped it I felt warmed up. Bindo doesn't know that I come to places like these. She would be scornful if she did. Not that she is a snob but she believed for a long time that I was fond of filth and uncleanliness. I can't deny it was only after knowing Bindo that I for the first time became aware of myself, so to speak. Before that I merely vegetated. It was only after Bindo that I started taking care of my appearance, of my clothes, of my hair.

I was feeling a bit feverish because of rain. In normal circumstances I would have taken to bed. But it seemed I had developed an unusual strength of will because of the new situation I had been confronting for the last two days. I had come up against a world where everything was unfavourable to me and the more I became aware of this the tougher I became.

But all one's strength and all one's will is often momentary and vulnerable to the slightest event, and all is chaos once again. Quite often one doesn't need any outward event—everything disintegrates of itself.

The boy at the tea shop increased the volume

of the radio. Ear-splitting film songs raged all around me while inside me there was a different kind of pandemonium. Suddenly I found myself struggling with some internal eruption that seemed to threaten the strength I thought I had only a moment ago. I made another effort to collect myself and crush the external noise as well as the internal laments as I sipped my tea wrapped in artificial calm.

I had taken off my coat and loosened my tie and even though it exposed me even more to cold it was better than bearing the burden of the wet coat.

It was already 2.30 p.m. but because of the weather one didn't realize it was so late. When I paid and came out of the tea shop the sky still looked unclear and pregnant with rain. The desolation of an afternoon can be most keenly realized only in Delhi where as soon the weather is fine people start milling around and the moment it becomes inclement they disappear God knows into what holes and corners.

By the time I reached home I had an oppressive sense of futility and of an all-encompassing void in which I was casting about in vain. Disgust is too inadequate for what I felt. It was beyond disgust. I don't know what it was.

My servant sat there, waiting for me or perhaps just dozing away. I don't know.

As I walked past him indifferently and entered the sitting room, I saw Bindo playing patience.

4

The sight of Bindo sitting there produced several simultaneous reactions: pride, scorn, satisfaction, anger and surprise! My face was visited by several shadows. Bindo gave me a look and continued to spread the cards around.

Without saying a word to her, I went in to change. I took my time in the bathroom and as I came out decked in clean, dry clothes, I saw she had packed away the cards.

I sat in a chair on the other side of the room, insultingly away from her. She looked the other way engrossed either in the calender on that wall or deliberately ignoring me.

"How long have you been here?"

"Not too long," she said without turning towards me.

I realized she was telling a lie. She must have come quite a while before. She must have come when it was raining. Her sari was still slightly wet. I had an impulse to ask her to take it off and dry it.

Inviting her to dinner at that time would have been a meaningless gesture.

"What will you have to drink?"

She held me with her eyes before saying, "I have already asked him for tea."

Her tone was casual. Presently the servant came with a tray full of tea things. He was about to put it down near me when she said, "Over here!"

She pointed to a table beside her. Obviously she didn't want to come over to my side of the room for tea.

I was a bit startled and alarmed by the note of authority in her voice. She started pouring tea without bothering about me. The servant looked at her, then at me, didn't understand what was going on, and left the room. I felt relieved at his departure. It wouldn't have taken him long to see that I was feeling humiliated.

The tea was ready. There were the two cups sitting unattended on the table. She couldn't decide whether she should pick up my cup and bring it over to me or wait for me to move. Courtesy demanded that I should get up and offer her a cup. But I chose to remain seated, indifferent to everything.

She had herself to blame for this awkwardness. She shouldn't have asked the servant to set the tea beside her. The dilemma she faced now would then have been mine.

A few moments went by before she looked at me through the corner of her eye. There was neither irony nor insult in her glance—it was meant only to size me up. I looked back at her unflinchingly. Soon she got up, brought my cup over to me and said, "Here you are!" And then she put a few biscuits on a plate and brought those over too and said, "Here you are!"

But she didn't come over all the way. She stopped short as if inviting me to get up and meet her half way. But I wasn't about to do anything of the sort. I had met her more than half way long ago. So I pushed my table over to her. She put my cup down, gave me a sharp look, went back to her seat, and started nibbling at a biscuit.

She began to look self-possessed once again. Tea had obviously started reviving her. She had a pullover on and she had wrapped it around tightly because of the cold but I could see she hadn't gotten rid of the chill caught in the rain. I got up and was about to place the heater closer to her when she said, "Don't bother, please. I can do without it." It meant she couldn't.

"Would you care for another cup?" she asked as she drained hers.

Her question reminded me that it was my place to ask that question of her for it was my home and my duty to play the host. But the way she had been carrying on would make one think it was her home and she was the hostess.

This self-assurance was new. Apparently she had acquired it in the intervening years. Not that she had not assumed authority in my home ever before, nor that it was the first time she had made me conscious of my own clumsiness. She had always been on the look-out to trip me. But she had never presumed so much before. What gave her the ground to take these liberties now? Or perhaps it is her intention to show that she had brought her ground with her.

If I had not known my Bindo I wouldn't have resolved the enigma. Even though she took me for an idiot I always knew she was anything but one. She had a point in everything she did or said. In order to present her point more precisely she often made use of subtle signals and hints.

Women have this thing—they hate a man who doesn't get their signals and hints.

"Would you care for another cup?"

She had started smiling on seeing me in a fix.

"No," I said brusquely.

She had started pouring herself a cup without waiting for my answer. The way she held her cup in her fine fingers suggested she hadn't weakened a bit, that despite everything she was all there. She looked happy as she sipped her tea. Even if there was any tension in her a few moments ago it had absolutely disappeared by now. It was impossible to guess from her looks that she had any problem of any sort.

I was curious but more than that I was envious of her naturalness—the way she sat sipping tea. The servant had looked in once to inquire if we needed anything. Or perhaps he only wanted to see what was going on. When he came in again, Bindo ordered him to clear away the tea things. The servant perhaps was even more astonished than I at Bindo's behaviour. He looked at her doubtfully for a moment and started picking up the things. As soon as he left, Bindo started tugging at her pullover.

I resolved not to break my silence. I wanted to torture her just as she had tortured me for years with her silence. But she had probably seen through my resolve to remain silent. And perhaps all she had come to do was to make me break my vow. Instead of risking her victory on this front I decided to change my tactics and challenge her on another.

"Why don't you change your clothes if you like? You look soaking wet."

She just pouted in reply.

"I think you should change your clothes or you'll catch cold."

I wanted to see how she'd react to that warning.

"To do that I'll have to go home."

I hadn't thought of that. She looked at me as if she was asking whether I wanted her to go home. I didn't want to give up so soon. But suppose she gets the better of me even on this front.

"You may go in and dry yourself if you like; it'll hardly take ten minutes; I'm afraid you'll catch cold otherwise."

"All right."

Her eyes glowed. As she got up she looked at me and I felt as if she had pierced into me and perceived my trick.

After she had gone inside I found myself a

bit embarrassed. Not because there was any question of modesty between the two of us. It wasn't the first time she had changed clothes in my presence. But I hadn't thought she'd agree to doing that so readily. I had hoped she'd resist and I'd succeed in embarrassing her.

From the noise inside I was sure she was really changing her clothes. In a little while she came out wrapped in a shawl.

"The sari wasn't all that wet and I have spread the pullover and blouse near the heater. I found this shawl over there."

She had wrapped the shawl tightly around her shoulders. The round spheres of her breasts under the tight shawl were unmistakable. As our eyes met I felt she had caught me stealing. She gave me the look of a victor and a very subtle smile swam across her lips.

This time instead of sitting away from me she planted herself in the sofa next to me. The closeness made me uneasy. Up till then I had sat with my legs stretched out and my feet on the arms of a chair. Now that she was next to me I thought I had to sit properly. The more I got caught in etiquette the more suffocated I felt.

It is very hard to resist the warmth of a body. But it wasn't just the warmth of her body; it was something else; the entire house seemed full of smoke and I saw no exit I could use.

She noticed I was uneasy. Her face reflected her pleasure at this. I gave her a sour look. Last evening I had not only quarrelled with her but had said enough to humiliate her in her own eyes. But the intervening years had if anything made her more smart. She pretended to have forgotten and forgiven my outburst of the previous day even as an elderly person would the folly of an adolescent. But I could neither forget the previous day nor forgive her. It is not in my nature.

I looked at my watch, like a big bureaucrat trying to brush off an ordinary visitor. But this wouldn't work with her. She sat there unperturbed. Or at least that is how she looked.

"It seems you have something special on your mind." Finally I had to break the ice. What I should have said was, "What brings you here?" But I controlled myself. She paid no attention to my remark. This is how she used to put me off—whenever she didn't want a confrontation she would pretend to be self-absorbed. After a couple of efforts she would come out of her shell—her eyes flashing scorn instead of defeat. I didn't want to repeat my question, for that would enable her to make me feel too ruthless or something.

But wasn't that exactly what I wanted? That she should realize that I could be ruthless too? After years of companionship and several attempts I had failed to impress upon her that I could be ruthless. And now that there was nothing between us, it was my chance. What shall I say then? "What brings you here?" How will she react to this? Will she mistake it for mere curiosity or will she understand that I am asserting my claim over my apartment.

There was a time when I used to try to adjust my behaviour and relationships according to what I read in books or heard from others. One has to be aggressive to show authority, compassionate to show love, bold to win praise, and so on. But none of this ever turned out to be true. Individual men and women have individual relationships. There are some similarities among them which give rise to cliches, but cliches work only as long as a man and a woman do not know each other. It is very hard to say whether knowing each other is coming close or drifting apart, for the closer one gets to someone the farther one goes: the more one loves, the more one hates. Loving is hating and hating is loving. The more one thinks about all this the greater the confusion and the first thing that is affected is one's self-assurance. And in the end one is left with nothing but an impaired self-assurance.

How can I claim that my treatment of Bindo was not motivated by impulses that had outwardly led to my victory but actually to utter failure.

"Did you say something?" She helped me out of my dilemma. Now if I liked I could ask, "What brings you here?" But something held me back, to my surprise, and I turned toward her. She was staring at me as if waiting for me to repeat my question. She didn't have a wrist watch on. Her wrists were covered by bangles. Normally she doesn't wear anything other than a plastic ring. This was the first time I had noticed her jewellery.

"It seems you have something special on your mind?"

"I do indeed." Her tone was so firm that I felt she had knocked me down. I wasn't prepared for such a sudden reversal.

I took a hold of myself and said, "Well?"

At this sign of my weakness she smiled and started playing with her bangles. Along with her bangles she was also playing with me. She knew she had put me down. Her smile became bigger. On noticing my irritation she turned aside a bit. Then she suddenly turned towards me and said, “I want my letters back.”

She had demanded those letters even before leaving me and I had refused. I had no attachment to those letters. There was nothing much in them. Over the years from here and there she had written to me. On reading them over I had realized there was no love in them but there was a lot of cunning. Everything was couched in caution. She had made no commitments whatsoever. And I wondered why on earth I had considered them as love letters. I would have returned them to her but she had left no address.

“So you are here to fight with me?”

“I have come to demand my letters back,” she said in an unruffled voice.

“I have none of your letters,” I said furiously.

“Who is fighting now?”

“I don’t care.”

“I won’t leave without my letters.”

“What do you think your letters are worth? Rubies and diamonds?”

“Why don’t you return them then?”

"Suppose I don't! What will you do if I don't?"

"I leave it to your imagination."

In the meantime she had got up from the sofa and gone and sat in the chair. She was fixing her hair now. The shawl had slipped off her shoulders and her breasts were almost bare. I had a beastly desire to grab her and throw her on the sofa and crush her underneath me. Suppressing this impulse to assault her, I said, "What do you think you are?"

Once again she ignored my remark and said, "My clothes will have dried by now." And she got up and walked into the bedroom. After a while when she came out her body looked even better. She had left the shawl inside but the top two buttons of her blouse were open so that her breasts still looked almost bare. I can't say whether she had done that deliberately or it was just carelessness, but I decided she was behaving like a whore.

"Apart from your letters didn't you leave many other things with me?" I had made up my mind to insult her and impress upon her that in my eyes she was no better than a whore.

"All I want back are my letters."

"But your letters are my property now."

"Nothing of mine can ever be your property."

"Are you demanding your letters back from others too or is it only from me?"

"What do you mean by others?"

I had finally hit the nail on the head.

"Are you trying to insult me?"

Obviously I had caught her weak spot.

"I should have expected that of you," she said with disgust.

I felt happy at her humiliation.

"There is nothing disgraceful in it. You have gone your way and I mine."

"What do you think is my way?" She was in a rage now.

I felt like saying, "The one that leads to hell!"

"Speak up, will you?"

She was trembling with rage. There was a time when at this point I would have softened and made up with her. But those days were over and in fact I was taking my revenge because of those days.

"Speak up, will you!" She was screaming now.

A woman is quite a silly thing come to think of it. She won't let you touch an inch of her but has no hesitation in assuming that she owns all of you.

Bindo stood up in her fury. It was obvious she had lost the battle.

"There is no point in screaming like this," I said without getting up. "I don't want any trouble."

"What do you want then?" she said as she sat down in the sofa. "Do you want to ruin me?"

"I don't want to ruin any one."

"Then why that false accusation?"

"Which false accusation?"

"When did you ever see me with someone else?"

"What do you want to prove? That you are a chaste Sita or Savitri?"

"Yes I am."

"No you are not!"

I was determined to argue to the end and to land her a crushing defeat for once. It wasn't easy to handle an obstinate woman like Bindo but what I had to do I had to do. She was capable of doing anything when enraged but I was not going to be daunted by that.

"Why don't you name the men I have been with?"

Her tone was rising once again. Her eyes were full of intense contempt and her nostrils wide with anger.

I couldn't help laughing, and she pounced upon me like an eagle.

"Are you playing with me? Aren't you ashamed of yourself? How can you play with a woman's honour? Am I a whore? I had never imagined you could fall so low!

Her voice was thick now and her eyes on the verge of water. I hadn't thought that what I had started would develop into this. I did want to enrage her but not to tears. Her crying used to upset me very much. I could not think of anything, other than winning her over by abject apologies. The more I apologized, the more she cried. Then finally a stage would be reached when she stopped crying and emerged glorious from her tears. This stage was then the end of the whole scene. I didn't want a repetition of that scene. If I offered even the faintest of apologies, everything would be destroyed.

And besides I hadn't hurt her unwittingly—I had done it deliberately. I should have been prepared for the consequences. In fact I should have foreseen them and thought of a strategy.

I kept quiet and gave her an opportunity to calm down. I looked at her. She had recovered herself. I lit a cigarette and thought perhaps the crisis was over.

But it wasn't. Had it been so, she would have left. But there she was, almost back to normal.

I decided that I should adopt her strategy. I should talk to her in the language of her choice but I should be the one to take the offensive. I decided the best thing would be to dismiss the servant, for even if his presence didn't seem to inhibit her, it did me. But I didn't want to be too obvious about it. That would have alerted Bindo and made him suspicious. So I went into the kitchen and asked him what he was cooking.

"What should I?"

"What do you have?"

"Eggplant, potatoes, cauliflower."

"Nothing more?"

"There wasn't much choice in the market."

"Go and get something else too."

"Such as?"

"Some more vegetables and fruit and fish."

I emphasized the fish for which he would have to go some distance.

As soon as the servant left, Bindo looked at me suspiciously. She might have seen something amiss. But she didn't seem to be afraid. Perhaps she too wanted us to be alone together. But as soon as we were alone I noticed a new reserve. It was already evening and in spite of the noise of the children in the street the atmosphere was somewhat tomblike.

Properly speaking Bindo should have left long ago, for after all we were no more than strangers. One gets bored with the company of a stranger after some time. But is she a stranger? Or is it that I desire her to become a stranger? I noticed a question on her face. She seemed to want to know what I had in mind.

"I want my letters," she said softly but firmly. Perhaps she had quietly realized that she had been wrong in screaming. She is one of those women who never expose their own weaknesses but manage to induce others to expose theirs.

Now I had no desire to keep her letters—they were no more than cobwebs in the house that I had not bothered to sweep away. But at the same time I didn't want to bow to her will.

"I would have returned those letters to you right then but for…"

"But for what?"

"But for the way you treated me."

"How was the way I treated you?"

There was firmness in her tone, and a sly satisfaction.

"You humiliated me."

"How?"

"You spread stories about me."

"What stories? Why don't you be more specific?"

"You know what I mean!"

"You know what you mean!"

I was alarmed at the irritation in her tone. Perhaps she was getting ready for another round. Now I was not afraid of fighting. On the contrary I wanted to fight. But I didn't want her to get the upper hand.

"When it had been decided that we couldn't carry on, why did you go and talk about our private affairs with others?"

I had not hoped that I would succeed in making her feel guilty but I had hoped that for a moment her mask would lift and I would see the old memories working but I was wrong. She sat there like a stone.

When there is new light on old things, one discovers that either the light is false or those old things were. After our separation whenever I thought of Bindo objectively I decided she was a neurotic. This would give me supreme satisfaction. Then one day I remembered what she had said once, "If I stay with you any longer I'll go insane." This upset me for several days and I kept wondering whether I was the cause of her neurosis and whether she was feeling better after leaving me.

I turned the other heater on because it had

grown colder. Now I could feel my feet and calves warming up.

"I don't need it," she said sharply. She must have thought I was trying to appease her. But all I was doing was to give her some time to come up with an answer.

"You haven't answered my question?" I said.

She turned away from me. She didn't want to face me. This suited her because she could offer an explanation without really confronting me. That is the way of experienced and smart girls.

That is what entices a man to begin with.

"Didn't you go and complain to Anil?" I wasn't going to be put off by her obduracy.

"I did," she said in an I-don't-care tone.

"Why did you tell him I had used you?" And when she didn't answer I added, "Can you tell me how I had used you?"

She raised her eyebrows as if to ask, "Do you want to fight?" I didn't want to fight but I didn't want to lay down my arms either, for any sign of slackness in front of an experienced fighter like Bindo would have been disastrous, as I knew to my cost.

"What has he got to do with it?" she asked sharply.

"Who is he?"

"Anil."

"I don't know."

"Then why do you keep invoking him?

"Because you went and told him everything."

"So I did. But it was necessary at the time."

"What do you mean?" I shouted.

"Otherwise there would have been a misunderstanding between you and me."

The seriousness of her face put me in doubt. Did she really want that there should be no misunderstanding between us? But what was there to misunderstand? She had come to know me more than I knew her. Without being married to me she had all the opportunities of weighing me and I had all the occasions whereby a man evaluates a woman.

It was dark in the room. I got up and switched on a light. She was looking for something in her handbag.

"Has the servant come back?" she asked.

"No."

"I need a glass of water."

She had two tablets of anacin on her palm.

The tone in which she asked for water surprised me. Was this the same woman who some time back had sat there making tea? And now she couldn't get up and get herself a glass of water?

"Tea will be better with those," I suggested.

"No, I don't want tea."

"They won't be very effective with water."

I was hungry and wanted some tea myself. When she kept quiet I got up and put the kettle on. I turned on the lights and went into the bathroom. After washing my face as I looked in the mirror I was startled. I saw a stranger's face. It was dark. It was my face of many years ago, of the day when Bindo and I had split apart. That was a day of tension exactly like today, a day of reckoning and restlessness. And I had the face of a beaten man. And today again the wax on my face had melted and the real features had emerged. I switched off the light in panic and came out hurriedly.

The servant had apparently come back from the market. Like before he had brought the tea tray and put it near Bindo. I was furious. But all I could do was to curse him quickly.

Bindo poured tea but unlike before she didn't offer it to me. She swallowed her tablets and started sipping her tea. When I offered her biscuits she said she didn't want any.

"How many people will be there for dinner?"

The servant came in and raised this clumsy question.

I should probably have shouted at him but I felt like commending him, for his question, I thought, would embarrass Bindo. The thought of her embarrassment gave me strength. Before, however, I could even snub him for form's sake, Bindo flashed an eye at me and turning toward the servant ordered him, "Only one."

The servant was intimidated by Bindo's stiff tone and he left without another word. Bindo knew how to save or spoil the situation. She not only knew how to save herself from embarrassments, she also knew how to help me out. She had herself humiliated me several times but she could not tolerate any one putting me in any awkward position. She had, it seems, kept her social graces intact. But my motives were always different. If I ever saved her from humiliation it was because I loved her, and if I humiliated her it was because I hated her. She knew that now I wouldn't be hurt by her humiliation; that is why she had not waited for me to help her.

Tea seemed to have braced her up. Wiping her lips with her tiny handkerchief, she asked, "What time is it?"

"Six."

"I should be going."

She hadn't said, "I'm leaving," which is what she says when she is angry.

I hadn't yet finished my tea. She seemed to be waiting for me to do so, so that she could leave. When she saw me lingering over it, her face narrowed a bit but then she managed to make herself natural again.

"Please give me my things."

I got up. Her letters were lying in my wardrobe. Tied in a handkerchief. I had taken them out a couple of times along with my clothes. They had acquired an animated antiqueness. The writing had faded and the paper had almost yellowed. I hadn't felt like taking them out recently but I had thought of them a few times. As I took them out I wondered if I was doing the right thing, for after returning those letters to Bindo I'd have no weapon left. Would I be able to confront her all by myself? Those letters were the only place where perhaps Bindo's real image was preserved. I felt like bluntly refusing to return the letters, "Look, I won't return them; you may do what you will." And I knew she could not do much more than scream in protest.

Watching me near the wardrobe, Bindo

remained skeptical. But as I took out that pink bundle and shut the wardrobe she felt relieved. I resumed my seat, holding that little bundle in my hand. Even the handkerchief had lost some of its original colour. So many years had gone by. The handkerchief also belonged to her. It gave off a damp odour. I felt like shouting, "This too is yours."

She was watching me closely. After a long pause she gave me a questioning look, "Do you want to strike a deal? I am ready even for that."

But I didn't want to strike a deal. I have never struck a deal about my emotional relationships. Relationships have always been relationships to me. I can't let them deteriorate into anything else. Bindo could take possession of her letters and be free. I didn't want to hold her against her will. Her main charge against me was that I had engaged her. Now that she had broken out of the cage, I couldn't have held her even if I wanted to. But at the same time I didn't want to accept defeat or her terms. Those letters were my property. I own them. She can't claim them back. If I surrender to her just because she insists, I'll be once again at her mercy.

I started tightening the knots of the bundle

absently. She gave me a puzzled look as she said, “It’s getting late.”

“I want to have a few things out with you first.”

Suddenly her face changed and her entire personality looked terrifying. Her nostrils started flaring and she got up, holding her handbag in one hand and her handkerchief in the other.

Seeing her in that state I was weakened at once. My hold on that bundle slackened and the damp odour became even more prominent. If I don’t keep my wits about me, something awful may happen, something really awful.

I got up and started pretending I was looking for a large envelope or something. “Let me wrap them for you properly.”

“That’s not necessary. After all this handkerchief also belongs to me.”

I fixed the bundle a bit in its handkerchief anyhow. She called the servant and asked him to go and get a taxi or a scooter. The servant looked scared by her harshness. After he left, she sat down.

The bundle was still in my lap. I didn’t know how to hand it to her. Should I just place it near her, or offer it to her, or get up and literally hand it over to her? There was no give and take between the two of us. There was nothing but estrangement. Finally I extended the bundle to her and said, "Here! Count them. They are over hundred in number I suppose."

I had thought she would grab them but she sat on unconcerned.

"Here, count them!" I repeated.

She put out her hand and took the letters. As she stuffed them in her handbag, she looked at me. There was anguish in her eyes. My fingers had trembled while handing the letters over to her.

As long as one has one last thing in hand there is hope. It is a false hope but it is there and it sustains one—may be there will be another day. One torment that I have always suffered is the torment of waiting. But had I been waiting only for that day? Did I have to break that last bond? Although years had gone by since our separation I had never really felt that our separation was final. After I had given those letters back to her that day I felt that it was final. In a moment Bindo had become a total stranger for me.

Now her presence there was putting me in a panic. We sat face to face but I couldn't look her in the eye.

I had been deceiving myself all that time. After

all why had I saved those letters? Was I attached to them? Did I feel a sense of obligation? Or was it only because I had hoped that sooner or later she would come back because of those letters and there would be another chance for us to repair the bridge that had broken between us? But if that was so, why had she demanded those letters so insistently? It was her fault. If she had wanted she could have forgotten those letters or not stuck to her demand.

I was feeling regretful but I didn't want to accept that the fault wasn't Bindo's but mine. She will again suffer because of her stubbornness. Like that other time. Even then I had tried to put off the crisis but Bindo's single-tracked mind had destroyed everything. But isn't it possible that this time it is my mind that is single-tracked? For all I know Bindo really wants those letters back. In that case she can't be blamed for anything. If she really doesn't feel anything for me, why should she leave any trace behind?

Because of cold she had pulled her sari tightly round her shoulders and was warming her hands at the heater. It was an unusually wretched evening. All around us there was stony silence. I felt as if I was in a primitive cave and there was no trace of human life anywhere near.

Suddenly the phone rang and the silence became even more unbearable. It was a wrong number. I thought maybe it was someone for Bindo, that she might have given someone my number and on hearing my voice the other party had pretended it was a wrong number. But the other party was a woman.

"Do you want to phone anyone?" I asked.

The oddness of this question and the formality of my tone obviously offended her. She said curtly, "No."

"But if you have to, feel free to use the phone."

"I have told you I don't have to."

She had understood how my question was related to the ringing of the phone. "No one will ever phone me here!" Her tone suggested I was the enemy and nobody would ever call her at my number.

I was beginning to feel annoyed once again. I felt I was being bitten by ants. I started cursing her in my mind, "You whore! You can't leave here after humiliating me! You vixen!"

"Perhaps you are in a hurry to go back to Regal?" I had underlined Regal as if it was a whorehouse.

She burst into a laugh. Perhaps she wanted

to make me realize I didn't know how to fight. But that should be no news to her. Her laughter couldn't have extinguished my anger. In fact it added to it because it came across as ridicule. For a moment I felt I was an idiot but the next moment my ego was hurt and my fury returned with double force.

It happens again and again. I try to rise above my hatred of her but after a while I come down with a crash. I try to reason with myself and calm down a bit; but then something happens to upset me and I am back in my world of anger and hatred. I had resolved to remain calm and teach her a lesson that day. But on the contrary she had succeeded in putting me down again. Every time I take a pledge to get back at her and put an end to my inadequacy but when it is all over I feel as inadequate as ever. And all I am left with is pain and despair and frustration. Will I always suffer and sulk like this? Will I never get out of this hell? I was feeling soft and sentimental and I didn't want to. Not before Bindo. For that would arouse all her innate aggressiveness and inflame her hatred.

She was still laughing. Obviously she was no longer worried about anything. In fact she had taken out her nail polish and was polishing her nails. Seeing her so self-absorbed made me feel envious of her. She was happy. Unperturbed.

The servant came in and announced he had brought the taxi. The way he addressed Bindo suggested he had been completely cowed down by Bindo. When she made no move to get up he repeated he had brought the taxi.

"I heard you," Bindo said casually and continued to polish her nails. Was she deliberately lingering or did she want to finish what she had started before getting up? Without raising her head she asked, "How is Anil?"

"I don't know."

It wasn't necessary to answer her but every time she succeeded in irritating me into a quick answer.

"What is he doing these days?"

I kept quiet I couldn't understand why all of a sudden she had started asking me about Anil. Is it another of her tricks? Or is it that she wants to convey she hasn't seen him since her return? What difference does it make to me even if she has met him? I don't care whom she meets or where she goes!

"Well?" she muttered.

"I told you I don't know."

"But don't you see him?"

"I do."

"Well then?"

"Well then what?"

"What is he doing these days?"

"He's doing a job. But I am not his keeper, you know!"

She smiled as she got up. I didn't stand up to bid her goodbye. I was through with bogus rituals. I was not going to be polite to someone I hated. Besides I hadn't invited her over. She had come on her own, against my wishes in fact, and was leaving after a quarrel. She had intruded into my house and been aggressive. The least I could do to punish her was to insult her.

I sat in my chair like a bureaucrat and looked at her coldly. She still stood there. I would have loved to throw her out if I could. She looked at me as if she was asking whether I wanted to throw her out. Suddenly she flared up and her body lit up like lightning as she took a step to the door and said, "I hadn't come for my letters!"

She stopped at the landing. I had a momentary desire to get up and go over to her. But I felt rooted to the spot I was sitting in. I heard her footsteps as they faded while she climbed down three storeys.

I felt as if some horrible mishap had taken

place and I was paralysed. What had happened was irrevocable. There wouldn't be another chance. Was it what I had wanted? I didn't know what I had wanted.

I got up and shut the window. But it seemed I couldn't keep the fog out. In spite of the light everything was indistinct—walls, rug, books, even I. In fact, I was the most indistinct of all.

5

Thirty-six hours had gone by but nothing had changed. It had cleared up a bit; the sky was sunnier and the atmosphere lighter, but my own depression was still there.

All that time I had remained shut up in the apartment. I didn't feel like stirring out, not even out of my bed. I tried to get rid of my agitation by reading or pacing the room but in vain. The confrontation had left an oppressive gloom. Just as a death in the family gradually makes the air grim, the shadow of that crisis had everything in its grip.

I had hoped that Bindo's departure would be followed by my freedom from love, hate, humiliation—everything. After all it was for this freedom that I had set the whole trap from the very beginning. But a trap attracts a counter-trap. Perhaps it hadn't taken Bindo long to realize that I was trying to trample her and win my own freedom.

Instead of becoming free I felt trapped more than ever. All my desires seemed to have deserted me and the entire inner strength seemed drained. It is only after one suffers a defeat in some individual struggle that one realizes how bookish is all that fantasy of regaining one's own universe, of returning to one's self.

An indefinable misery had besieged me from all sides. I wasn't being bothered by the relationship that had died; the real source of my torment was the violence of the shades that had suddenly started rising in my own inner inferno.

Had it been mere exhaustion, I would have overcome it. But it was neither disgust nor despair. Gradually I had begun to understand that it was a torment that one had to undergo sooner or later.

It wasn't that my love for Bindo was beginning to revive or that the memories of that love had returned. Nothing but tension and torment had survived by way of memories. There was no question of my becoming contrite or compassionate towards Bindo. That kind of bond between the two of us had ended long ago. My bitterness hadn't abated. I hadn't even been able to hide that. It had in fact inevitably spilled out. Not that I was feeling any lighter. I was aware that poison never dies. It may change its form, it may play some tricks, but it never dies.

So I had passed those thirty-six hours lying in bed, pacing the room, or sitting in the sun. Every moment had been heavy. I wouldn't have hesitated to go out and buy some peace of mind if it were available in the market. One can't expect anyone else to break one's shackles but I wonder if one can do so by oneself. I don't know. What I do know is that I am more bound than ever. Whatever I do results in the walls of my prison rising a bit higher. After years of encirclement I had started realizing for the first time that day that perhaps I had no being of my own.

After lunch I was lying in the sun when I heard someone coming up. It was Anil.

"What is the matter?" he said as he noticed my listlessness. He was all dressed up. "Come on, get up," he said, patting me on the back. "You won't go to heaven doing this."

His tone was very casual but I was suspicious. He looked happy as he sat there in the sun. Just by looking at him one could tell that it was Sunday.

"Why are you lying down like that? I feel lousy just looking at you."

He was in a playful mood. And in fact I was happy that he had dropped by.

"Have you eaten?" he asked as he covered his eyes with a magazine.

"Yes. How about you?"

"Yes. I ate just before stirring out."

"What are you up to?"

"Oh, nothing much. May go to the movies provided I get a ticket." He paused and continued as if he was talking to himself. "Perhaps I will get one in black."

I turned on my side so that the sun now warmed my back and gradually my mood like my body was also getting warmer.

"Would you like to come along?" he asked as he released a big cloud of smoke.

For a moment I felt like saying yes. It would pass the time. But then the desire died. I kept quiet.

"It is up to you. I'm sure we'll manage to get tickets somehow. "

He was still worrying about tickets. That seemed to be his biggest problem just then. Isn't he lucky? I turned on my side and saw that he was staring at me. I had failed to peer behind his words but he was trying to look beyond my silence. He smiled as our eves met.

"Come on!"

I got up but I didn't really want to go. Was he enjoying my misery or was he being friendly? He saw through my suspicion.

"I sort of depended on your coming along."

We got up and went into the living room. He looked at his watch a couple of times. This was an obvious hint to hurry up.

"Some other day. I don't feel like it today."

"Well, I guessed as much. But I thought what the hell. It would have diverted you some."

I came down the stairs with him to see him off. Others' pity quite often is an affront to one's own being. But there are moments when someone's pity wins you over completely. I felt deeply grateful to Anil at that moment. He seemed sincere. Obviously, he knew the hell I was in and he couldn't help coming over to help me. But that wasn't the way out for me. I knew that my gloom wouldn't leave me no matter what I did or where I went. Nobody in the world could help me.

We crossed the street over to a betel-leaf shop. Both of us needed cigarettes. Everything seemed relaxed. Behind that shop some people were busy with a card game. On the big patch of sun near the two-storeyed house a bunch of boys were jumping around. Nobody seemed to be troubled about anything.

Now Anil came a bit closer to me and said in a very warm tone, “Bindo was quite unhappy.”

This meant he knew everything. She must have seen him. Normally I would have felt offended at that. But just then I wasn’t. Neither at her breach of confidence nor at the fact that he knew all about us.

“When did you see her?”

“Day before yesterday.”

“When?”

“After she was with you.”

“What did she say?”

“Not much. But she was unhappy.” After a pause he continued, “All she said was, ‘I don’t know whom he is torturing—himself or me!’”

I could well imagine Bindo saying that.

“I am afraid you misunderstand her.”

This meant she wasn’t quite indifferent yet. Or it could be yet another of her strategems.

“I’m afraid you are creating complications where there aren’t any.”

Anil left after this. It would have been a lot easier for me if it was only a question of unnecessary complications. But the mess I was in was beyond my control.

I had to do something. On getting back to my place I changed clothes. Just as a suicide is driven by some superhuman will-power into a state of mind free of all doubts, I too was suddenly relieved of all reasoning. I didn't know what I was about to do, nor did I want to know what I should do. All that I knew was that I had to do something.

As I came out I started walking absentmindedly. If only I could walk on indefinitely I wouldn't have arrived at conclusions which perhaps were my destiny. As I reached within a short distance of Bindo's house I had a hesitation but I was easily able to overcome it.

It wasn't the resolution of a victor though but the self-respect of a victim. There was no other way to defend myself. I couldn't retreat because behind me was a wall that could have broken my head. I didn't know what was in front of me. Maybe nothing but darkness.

I had thought I'd find her sitting on the lawn, knitting or just enjoying the sun. But she had gone out. The servant told me she had been out since morning and hadn't come back for lunch.

I was wondering what I should do next when

her servant started cheering me up. He said she should be back any minute now, for it was rare that she kept away from home so long; in fact it was the first time she had done so. And then he gave me a questioning look as if he wanted me to tell him why she had done that.

As I took a seat in her room I saw my picture, in a frame, sitting in a niche unstained by dust or by rain. It looked like it had been well taken care of during all those years. As I looked at that picture I felt I had nothing to do with it. It was some other man who was keeping an eye on me, the intruder.

The servant came in several times just to be around in case I wanted anything. I didn't ask for anything but after a while he came in with coffee. He must have recognized me from my picture and concluded I was somebody special. Nobody but an old servant knows better who is special and who is not.

After he left I examined the room at leisure. There hadn't been any increase in things. A few books including some old textbooks and a few volumes of current Hindi and English fiction, a Buddha, an ashtray, a few cushions, a few nice chairs. In household matters Bindo was no different from any ordinary woman. All that was lacking was a money plant. Otherwise that room could have belonged to anyone living in Delhi. After all those years and travels she hadn't brought about any change in her style. I was surprised.

The adjoining room was her bedroom. Every time the curtain moved I could see everything—bed, wardrobe, an almirah, everything. Just two rooms. This place was much smaller than her old place. But she had a little lawn here. Perhaps she had moved because of the lawn. Or maybe there was some other reason. She didn't need a place all that big.

Outside on the lawn, the sun was receding. As the afternoon advanced, I became more lonely in that room. Bindo's servant came in once again. He looked worried. It meant he was a devoted servant and Bindo trusted him.

I got up and started browsing about her books. There was nothing but popular stuff. Then I noticed that bundle of letters on the shelf. My heart started beating faster and I felt like touching those letters. But I returned to my chair. I was surprised to see that she had left those letters around after all that quarrel over them. Did that mean that those letters were a mere pretext and that quarrel was for its own sake? Didn't she say before leaving that she hadn't come to me for those letters? Did it mean that I shouldn't have returned those letters? Did it mean that everything would have ended differently if I hadn't returned those letters?

I felt I had committed a mistake in coming over. I should have held back. My resolution began to falter. Would she visit me again if I left without seeing her? The thought of her visiting alarmed me as well as delighted me at the same time. I tried to think of something else and keep myself busy with the cold coffee in front of me.

When the servant came in to pick up my coffee cup I was suddenly reminded that Anil had seen her near Regal Cinema. Bindo had a lot of self-assurance but she wasn't the type to move about all herself. It was rather puzzling that she should have been out for such a long time.

"Does she go out quite often?"

"She goes out occasionally."

"Does she remain out this long?"

"Never more than an hour or two." He seemed to be answering my questions as well as his own.

"Is she generally with somebody or alone?"

Bindo's servant looked a bit startled at this

question but he recovered soon enough and said, "She goes out alone and comes back alone."

I shouldn't have asked him that but I didn't really regret doing that. I didn't feel that respect for Bindo which would have stopped me. Besides, it was rather difficult for me to believe that she wasn't with someone. It wouldn't do for her just to assert loudly that she hadn't been unfaithful.

It is painful to think that a woman one has been with is now with someone else. Men like me are tormented by envy too. At the same time ever since her departure I have wanted to catch her with another man. She has always managed to escape being caught. I want that at least once I should catch her so that she can't look me in the eye. So far I had had no luck.

I heard a scooter outside. It was Bindo. I hurriedly picked up the first book I saw and pretended to be absorbed in it. I wanted to postpone the confrontation as long as I could. My resolve to be unafraid notwithstanding, as I heard her steps, my heart started beating like the heart of a man who after having been fired from his job is waiting for his boss in the boss' office.

Bindo was startled to see me. Her eyes flared up. I was a bit unnerved lest she should start shouting at me. Suppose she orders me to get out of her house! If at all I knew her she wouldn't do that. But things had happened during the past several days and I hadn't forgotten those.

She passed by me and went into the adjoining room. She had some paper bags, maybe fruit or something, in her arms. She had an exquisite Kanjeevaram sari on and her face looked radiant. She put on beautiful clothes only when she was happy.

She came out of the bedroom with the same sari on. There was a smile on her lips. I couldn't make out why she was so happy. There was no trace of bitterness anywhere. Or perhaps all her anger and bitterness were only for my benefit and away from me she was at peace. It doesn't take much to make women happy—shopping, movies, flowers, kisses, anything will do.

As she perched on a table at some distance from me she gave me a self-assured look, as much as to convey that she knew I would be there sooner or later. I felt a bit embarrassed at that look and, seeing through my unease, she said casually, "I went out for shopping and decided to lunch out; that is why it took me so long."

There was no need for this explanation nor had I expected it. But perhaps she wanted to reassure me. I cast a "never mind" glance at her, and before I could say that I had already had a cup of coffee, she walked over to the kitchen and ordered coffee.

I noticed that her bearing was if anything full of greater self-confidence than before. She sat closer to me this time and cast an eye on that bundle of letters on the bookshelf. I started turning the pages of that book in my lap when I saw her doing that. On looking up I saw she was smiling. I was a bit touched by the warmth of that smile. Now she was looking straight and full at me.

"I owe you an apology for that day," I said in a slightly quivering voice.

I had said that in a guileless way. Of course I hadn't meant to placate her. Just as the first thing a blind man bumps into becomes his destination for that moment, similarly Bindo had become my destination. At that moment I was neither happy nor unhappy about Bindo. But I was still resentful.

As soon as she heard me apologizing, her eyes were ablaze. The eyes that only a moment before were full of warmth were suddenly violent. As if she was saying that the man who had misbehaved that day was some other man and not I. I had made a *faux pas.* Perhaps I shouldn't have reminded her of that day. Even though her fury had dissolved in no time, it wasn't that easy for her to regain her composure. As she held the coffee cups, her hands trembled.

I felt like repeating my apologies to help her regain her composure but the need didn't arise. Soon enough she was normal and stirring sugar in my cup with the same warmth with which she had greeted me. Stirring sugar in each other's cup generally presupposes a great degree of closeness between two people. I was a bit alarmed at the intimacy and confidence with which Bindo was stirring my cup. I picked it up and had a hot, quick sip.

"The price of everything has gone up," Bindo said. "The meanest of slippers costs no less than fifteen rupees now." And as she looked down at her feet, my eyes followed hers and I found myself gazing at her slippers.

"Every visit to the market means a hundred rupees gone. It must be hell for the poor!" Bindo seemed to be talking to herself. In spite of the intimate domesticity of her tone I was uneasy and felt trapped.

"Want another cup?" she asked like an accomplished hostess.

"No. Two cups of coffee were more than enough for me."

"Would you like to sit outside?" she asked as she poured herself another cup.

When I didn't come up with any answer she answered her own question, "Maybe it is all right here; the sun is going away anyway." She drew the heater closer to me. I was reminded that two days ago when I had put the heater closer to her she had withdrawn her feet as if they had been scorched. Now she seemed to be opening like a sunflower as she sat near the heater.

"Have you read that book?" she asked pointing to the *Pickwick Papers* lying in my lap.

I had no interest in that book. Moreover her question was quite silly. Women can't avoid being silly whenever they start talking about literature and art; more often than not they say something silly the moment they open their mouth. After all those years didn't she know that my whole life had been devoted to reading?

"Hmm," I said.

My answer was as professorial as her question was elementary.

"Let me change into something else," she said as she got up and walked over to her bedroom.

The curtain had slipped to one side and exposed a lot more of her room to my eyes. I could have easily watched her changing her clothes in front of the mirror but I wasn't interested. I turned my face the other way.

"It's a small bedroom," she remarked as she came out. "Rents have soared so high. This little apartment costs me three hundred. But it has a good lawn."

She came and sat next to me on the sofa. She had put on a simple sari and washed away her make-up. That is how actresses are, I thought. They can change faces in no time—hate instead of love, anger instead of hate, compassion instead of anger, self-castigation instead of compassion, and so on. Bindo is indeed quite versatile and theatrical.

Now that she was sitting so close I could not ignore the body odour that I had known so well and that I had all but forgotten. Years ago whenever I felt a longing for her that odour used to emanate from my own inside. But for the past several years it had left me, just as one's taste leaves one's palate after a long illness.

I was even more ill at ease now that she was sitting so close to me. I picked up the same book and started turning the pages. Bindo of course had seen through my dilemma. She got up and turned the heater towards me and resumed her seat.

"You look unwell to me," she said suddenly. "How about an A.P.C.?"

I scanned her face to see if she was being sarcastic. Before she could get up and bring the medicine, I blurted out, "Not at all. I am perfectly all right."

"You don't look all right to me," she said fondly. "Let me feel your pulse."

Her hand was stretched toward mine. Obviously, she was being playful. I don't like this kind of playfulness. The moment she touched my arm, I withdrew it. She was ridiculing me. I had come to her house—in anger or in remorse or whatever—but she had no right to ridicule me. She was treating me the way forward girls treat a shy young man. She knows I am not that shy. It is just one of those situations—and she should not be mean and take advantage of me because of that. And I should have known that. Bindo had a mean streak even if she had her generous moments.

I was quite incensed by her move. She had challenged my self-respect and masculinity. The same hands that she seemed to be making fun of had peeled off her petticoat, fondled her high breasts and held her so many times.

She got up and went into the bathroom, maybe because of embarrassment. But I was wrong. Girls like Bindo are never embarrassed. They know how to embarrass others. They can ensnare you in such a way that there is no way out.

The first time we had met she suggested we should hire a scooter to wherever we were going. I was a bit puzzled but when the scooter began to throw us in each other's lap I understood why she had preferred that to a cab. If it had not been a scooter, she would have thought of some other way. On our second meeting she invited me to read her palm. I don't know how to read palms nor do I believe in palmistry. But the way she had put it I had to pretend that I knew palmistry. She knew I was pretending and I knew she knew I was pretending. Thus we had started with a lie. Perhaps everybody starts with a lie. Perhaps without a lie no one would know how to start.

During that bumpy ride in the scooter with her I almost gasped for breath and while reading her palm I couldn't control the shakes in my body. Not that I was a diffident young man even then. But one can't help being doubtful and diffident when one is about to fall in love. Love doesn't add to one's self-confidence; it renders one indecisive, uncertain, and helpless.

It was she who had taken the initiative and when the time came it was she who ended the relationship. She wasn't experienced but talent did for her what experience does for other women.

I cannot accept that I lacked manliness for I didn't—neither then nor later. Then what was it that constricted me, that bound me to her like a slave? I can't say. I don't know. Even those who claim to know everything know that certain things cannot be known. Everybody comes up sooner or later against a riddle he can't unravel. In my case it was Bindo.

As she came out of the bathroom she had a shawl round her shoulders.

"It is rather chilly here; let's go into the other room."

The other room meant the bedroom. I didn't mind even though that other room couldn't possibly be any warmer. It was dimly lit. Everything in there seemed asleep—bed, cushions, wardrobe and Bindo's picture on the table. For a moment it seemed I had entered a strange universe. One is slightly self-conscious on entering a woman's bedroom. I wasn't exactly self-conscious because it wasn't the first time I had gone into Bindo's bedroom. But my memories had faded. That is why at first it looked unfamiliar. But then soon enough everything began to look exactly as it had been.

On re-examining the room I realized that it was simple but not dreary or widowed; on the contrary it had the sharp attractiveness of an experienced woman's touch about it. A few things but tastefully displayed. It seemed to have been painted recently, perhaps around Diwali.

I sat down in a chair near the bed while she planted herself on a stool in front of me without any hesitation. I noticed that with age she had put on some weight even though at first sight she still looked slim.

She sat so close to me that her perfume seemed my own. She sat rather intently as if she was reading the lines on my face.

"Can't you let bygones be bygones?" she said all of a sudden. It was the first time she had actually uttered those words but her gestures and general behaviour had implied that much all the time. A question like that is normally conciliatory. But the tone in which Bindo had uttered it didn't suggest that. It seemed she had been irritated for a long time and had finally blurted it out.

The moment I heard her question, my ego came alive again. I became mindful of all the insults and humiliations she had subjected me to. I am used to answering every question in a straightforward manner. Sometimes I carry this practice too far and behave like a damn fool. So this time too I all but spat out "'I can't" but I was able to control myself.

She looked at me as if she was sizing me up. I didn't look away or down.

"I thought you'd have forgotten everything by now."

There was an ironic twist to her lips.

"What do you mean?" I said gathering all my strength.

"That is why I returned."

Bindo knew how to act. Whenever things reached a breaking point she would become contrite. But, at that moment, was she being contrite, or was she merely acting, or was she confessing candidly? It was hard to tell. Bindo had become such an expert in presenting pretense as truth that the difference between the true and the false had disappeared.

In any case I couldn't forget what I had gone through. It wasn't just a question of revenge. Revenge is easy. The difficult thing is to defend oneself without being revengeful. In a way she was right. I had forgotten the past. It was Bindo who had come and revived it. But for her return I wouldn't have recognized her. This was quite another confrontation, quite another crisis.

"I am incapable of nursing a grudge," I said before I could stop myself. I could have bitten my tongue. By saying that I had surrendered. Her eyes brightened up. As if that was what she was waiting for. I noticed it wasn't gratitude but a defiant and aggressive self-confidence produced by my confession.

But was it really my confession? Was it true that I was incapable of nursing a grudge? Didn't I hate her? Now I know that I didn't. I had this delusion that I hated her.

Now she was bending over me in such a way that her face was casting a shadow over mine. Her shins were about to touch my knees. I didn't stir in my chair. I merely tolerated her proximity.

Then she took my hand in hers and said, "Have you really forgiven me then?"

She spoke her part like an actress. I couldn't help laughing. Had it been another occasion she would have dropped my hand in a huff. But she held on this time. She had to.

Her hand was warm but I wasn't being responsive. It struck me that she was not only clever but also crazy. She was behaving quite crazily. How can one ever effect reconciliation like this? But she didn't want a reconciliation. All she wanted perhaps was to be with me.

"Well, have you forgiven me?"

There are moments when one hates one's limp body. I felt that my cold stinking hand was something slimy and dead. If I continued like that my whole body would be lifeless.

I tried to withdraw my hand but Bindo didn't let go. She made her grip stronger.

I hadn't said anything definite. The conclusions she had arrived at were her own. How could she have concluded that everything had been resolved when for the past few days I had been trying to impress upon her that nothing had been resolved.

She got up abruptly and wrapped her shawl properly around her shoulders.

"Shall I ask him to set the table?"

I was flabbergasted. I wasn't a guest in her house. The circumstances of my visit wouldn't even admit of formal politeness. She had no reason to be so warm and hospitable. I felt trapped. Yield an inch and she'll take a mile. But I could if I wanted to step back and be free again.

"No. I won't have dinner here?" I said brusquely. Women feel challenged by this kind of brusqueness and become even more persistent. In order to avoid that I softened up a bit as I added, "I have a dinner appointment with someone."

Bindo knew when I was lying just as she knew everything else about me. She held me with her eyes as she said, "Well, you can ring up and cancel the appointment. Unless of course it is something special."

She looked at me questioningly as she stood by me. Then she said, "Shall I bring the phone over?"

I knew she was being ironic. I lowered my eyes.

She returned a moment after she left the room as if she had forgotten to ask me something. She had but what she asked me was so unexpected that for the first time I felt she had cast herself into an altogether different mould. So far she had only irritated me but now she was quite fearsome. One can never tell how a woman will blossom with time and circumstances. She with her sudden beauty and love was not only fascinating but also intimidating. It was almost like a minor explosion.

What she had come in to ask was what I would like to drink. I would never have expected this of her. Not that she hated drinking but she had always found my drinking quite intolerable. We fought whenever I drank. She used to sulk and be angry like a wife. Partly to establish her authority over me and partly to keep her ideal of a housewife alive she used to extract pledges from me that I wouldn't ever drink again. And the pity of it was that I only drank on rare occasions when I had to because of social obligations. As a matter of fact she often made me swear that I would give up smoking also. Every woman needs to do things like this to convince herself that she is a woman. And it is these demands of women born as they are of their egotism which attract men to them because they remind them that they are not meant only for themselves, that some other person has the right to encroach upon their selves.

Before I could say yes or no, her servant had come in and placed everything near us. He didn't even look straight at me, as if this new turn had intimidated him even more.

"Go get some ice," she ordered him sharply. Then she realized her mistake and said, "Forget it. Bring some warm water."

An unopened bottle of rum stood between us.

"Who was it meant for?" I asked. My curiosity was quite natural.

She looked at me as if my question was quite silly. Didn't you know that sooner or later you would come here and be treated like this? Are you really so unfamiliar with this vocabulary of welcome? I too am new to this.

No one knows one's own destiny. And no one is more awesome than the one who knows yours. Bindo had known mine for years. As I looked up at her she looked my destiny incarnate.

As I poured myself one I looked at her to find if she wanted one too. She just smiled. Drink never gives me any pleasure and I never drink for pleasure. It just warms my nerves and quickens my pulses. After a few sips as I eyed her I saw she was enjoying the scene. Her fingers were dancing in fact. Out of embarrassment at having been caught by surprise, she said, "What time is it?" And then embarrassed at her question she said, "Never mind. What's the hurry!"

I knew she was in no hurry. She had

understood that every cycle took us to a point beyond which we could not go. She knew that I was doomed. And so did I as soon as she had returned. Like a sick man who knows when his death is near.

But drinking delayed that death a little. It revived all my resentment even as it inflamed my body. All my anger and hatred for Bindo broke out. I poured myself another drink quickly. Now is the time! I'll never get this chance again! I began to prepare my attack as I got drunk. Now is the time to humiliate her, to trample over her, to break her! The idea of her breaking gave me pleasure.

"Cigarettes?" I demanded. My own had run out long ago and I needed one badly.

Bindo dug about and produced a pack of cigarettes in no time. So she had thought even of that. But this was no occasion for appreciating her. I had to expose her. I must step forward and do it. Now.

"Mean!" I said with relish.

"What?" she asked with a start.

"You are mean!" I said without flinching.

There was a flicker of violence in her eyes but then she held herself in check and started to laugh.

"You can't rush me a second time!"

"Can't you let bygones be bygones?"

"I can't."

I had hoped this would infuriate her and everything would be fine. But she remained composed. There was a hint of hurt in her eyes. Perhaps she did feel hurt by what had happened.

"Dinner is ready."

But I was prepared for this. "I am not here for your dinner. I want to have it all out with you."

She didn't reply. Her face showed agitation. She was obviously not prepared for this. She had never thought I would start stripping her bare like that. She was at a loss for a proper response. Even if she had wanted she couldn't escape the consequences of the situation that had been created. After years I felt I had the upper hand.

"Look, if you think we can get together again you are mistaken. Nobody can love a woman like you. You are an emasculator. You are too vain. You have no regard for anyone else. The time I spent with you was like hell for me. And I was lucky that somehow I got out of that hell. Why have you come back? Why don't you let me be? If you don't leave, I will!"

These were bitter words. Any other woman would have been broken by what I had said. A weak woman would even have been destroyed for ever. But Bindo is an experienced woman. The more I shouted the tougher she looked. Just as I ended my outburst she got up and said, "Dinner will get cold. Come on. You can say all this tomorrow morning."

I felt like screaming, "I want to say it now, this moment!" and give her a resounding slap. But she was offering me support to stand up. She wanted to make me feel that I was drunk. This was one of the many ways she knew of demoralizing me. Of course I was drunk but certainly I could do without her support.

I brushed her aside and poured myself another drink. Then I downed it at one go. Up until then there was fire in my stomach; now my intestines were also inflamed.

As I walked to the bathroom I felt unsteady but was able to manage thanks to my reflexes.

"I am not hungry," I said as I sat down at the table. I had told a lie. I had been feeling hungry for quite some time and drink had intensified it just as it had everything else.

"He's quite a good cook. Before this he was at several good places including an embassy."

She kept bringing me back to dinner. I could see she didn't want me to resume our old topic.

Perhaps women shed all hostility while feeding a man. Their love overflows when they are serving food. I'd go to the extent of saying that it overflows only when they are serving food. Bindo was putting various vegetables on my food with such affection and concentration that I couldn't help appreciate it. But I had become quite cunning by now; I suppressed my appreciation.

It was quite a banquet. Perhaps she had ordered the servant to do something special. The food had in it the touch of a woman. Every now and then she kept loading my plate with everything.

It must all be a fraud. A mere show. Pretense! She is only play-acting. She thinks I am an idiot. But I have had my revenge. Not once, not twice, but thrice. Now I won't feel sorry that I didn't do anything. But even now I have a residue of resentment. That will always be there. I can't do anything about it. Nor can she. The way she has destroyed me has left in me an ineradicable desire to retaliate.

As I got up from the dining table I cast a casual look at the walls of the room. They didn't show any signs of affluence; all they displayed was the incompleteness of the middle class. I noticed the same incompleteness on Bindo's face too. She looked a bit worried because of my drunkenness. When she saw me scanning her, she put on another, more cheerful face.

My head was heavy. No sooner had I stood up than I felt like sitting down again. Somehow I walked into the other room and collapsed on the sofa. She came close and said, "Let me press your head awhile."

She is being sarcastic again seeing that I am in no condition to strike back. She won't miss a chance to put me down. I said nothing in answer to her offer but she continued to stand close to me. I felt like cursing her once again. Vain! Deceitful!

"Why don't you lie down awhile," she said as she pressed my forehead. "If you close your eyes maybe you'll get some sleep," she continued as if she was talking to a child.

My body had begun to sag and I was stretching myself on the sofa even though I didn't want to. I was afraid I had had a drop too much. It had happened before but not quite. Maybe it was not because of drinking but because of something else. The last thing I wanted was to be dependent upon her or that she should be in a position to take pity on me. But whatever I didn't want was happening to me.

She slipped a pillow underneath my head and now I was lying fully stretched. My eyes were dazzled by the light and all sorts of spots were shrinking and expanding in my subconscious. Aggression assumes nightmarish images when one is drunk. The only image I saw was of Bindo's destruction.

Intoxication had produced a frightening inner agitation. Everything looked dim and foggy. I was lying on the sofa like a cripple and at a short distance from me stood Bindo undressing herself. My presence didn't make any difference to her.

I shouldn't have been surprised for after all I had seen her undressing so many times. But after the relationship is over the wall of modesty arises once again. And then everything has to be done behind screens. Bindo had demolished that wall once again.

There are times when one wants to spit at the sky or to crush an ant or to scream. That was exactly how I felt as I lay there seething in the light. But instead of screaming I was quietly crying. I had turned my face to the wall so that Bindo shouldn't see. If I could I'd have strangled her.

I had been betrayed by my own will. I had

arrived at a point where I shouldn't have. I had become what I shouldn't have. I have had my moments of self-castigation but never before had I been so remorseful. My tears were only one manifestation of that remorse. There was a lot more that could not even come out. I had become quite helpless. All I needed to go over the edge was a slight push.

It was about midnight when I opened my eyes and found that I was lying not on that sofa I had earlier collapsed on to but on the foot of Bindo's bed. I was lying at Bindo's feet. Beside the bed there was a dim blue light whose reflection fell on the bed. She had come awake when I started stirring.

"How did I get here?" I asked expressionlessly.

"You kept saying you were sorry for a long time before collapsing here."

"What do you mean 'here'?"

"I mean here at my feet," she said in a scared tone. I could see fear in her eyes.

I broke my silence and asked, "What did I say?"

"All kinds of incoherent words," she said still in a frightened tone.

"What words? Why don't you tell me?"

"You kept apologizing. You kept saying, 'You

have never understood my love; you still don't.' I tried to talk you out of it but you kept falling at my feet and saying, 'Forgive me! Don't ever leave me! I can't live without you. I have tried and failed! You don't know how hard it has been for me all these years. I'll do whatever you say. Don't leave me.'"

She lowered her eyes and I did mine.

"Once I tried to put you to bed properly," she continued without looking up, "but you pushed me back and said, 'Let me lie here! This is all I deserve'. After you had fallen asleep I tried again but you pushed me away." She paused and said softly, "Will you forgive me?"

She must have taken off my coat and tie while I was asleep. "Do you have anything for a headache?" I said.

She got up and started opening a little attache-case. She was almost naked. All she had on was a petticoat and a blouse. I felt guilty. But she didn't seem to be so. The thought that I had been apologizing and that I had been sleeping in the same bed with her kept searing me. But how did it happen? How could I fall at her feet and beg her love when I hated her and wanted to crush her because she was so mean? Was it I or my shadow? I fell in my own estimation. I was sure I had fallen in hers too. If it is love that I want of her, will she ever give me that after she has seen me lying at her feet?

It is absolutely false that I can't do without her. I repeated this to myself like a charm or a lesson. But even as I did so I was doubtful. There was another voice inside that kept saying: This is the truth: you can't live without Bindo; stop torturing yourself.

I closed my eyes and tried to put everything aside. But as soon as I closed my eyes that accursed picture become even more distinct: me falling at her feet, begging her forgiveness, crying, everything!

A man can't fall lower than this! Even Bindo had found it unbearable. That is why she had tried to pull me up and make me sit straight. I put my hand on my forehead and felt that instead of exposing Bindo I had exposed myself.

"What are you thinking?" she asked as she gave me a tablet and a glass of water.

"Nothing," I said as I swallowed the tablet.

"You treat me as a stranger, don't you?" she said, looking soulfully into my eyes. "But all this time I wasn't asleep; I was worrying about you."

Maybe she was telling the truth. But I was in no mood for truth at that time. I didn't want to be convinced that she loved me. I was fighting my last battle.

She sat down beside me on the bed and put her arms round my neck.

"Look, why do you treat me as a stranger?"

Her tone was sincere. A woman's arms tell you clearly whether an embrace is true or false. The easiest thing to detect is the falsehood of an embrace. At that moment there wasn't a trace of falsehood in her touch. Besides, what the hell did it matter even if it was false.

Bindo lifted my chin with her finger and kissed me. When I didn't respond she said, "Forgive me. I know you feel hurt. I didn't want you to. But you brought it upon yourself."

When I still kept quiet, she got up and said, "Please forgive me. Look, I am willing to make amends."

She sat down and put her head on my feet. I got up abruptly and said, "No, that's not proper." I hadn't expected her to make amends in that way.

She was not responsible for the humiliation I had brought on myself by falling at her feet. She could if she liked hold herself indirectly responsible for it. But I couldn't do even that. I was responsible for whatever had happened. She had no reason to beg my forgiveness.

Whenever you lift a suppliant woman she expects you to take her in your arms. After having been thus lifted she rises to a human status and subsequently in love she achieves an equal status. I should have raised her and given her that status but I recoiled from her as if she was a corpse at my feet.

For a moment she looked quite furious. Then she got up. Apparently she had understood my dilemma and realized that I wouldn't be able to rise to the occasion, that she would have to do it instead.

Silence froze between us once again. The clock sitting on the table ticked and its dial glowed. Its pointed hands pierced not only my eyes but my insides. Outside the window was a dark lawn. There was a narrow circle of light on the street.

"It's very cold today," she said and shut the window with a loud thud. Then it was the same sinister silence once again.

"Switch off the light," she said.

"Let it be."

I would be nowhere without that light, dim as it was.

Bindo had stretched herself out fully on the bed. I still sat there. I would have got up and sat on the chair but it was too cold.

Bindo extended her hand and pulled me toward her.

"Come on, do lie down," she coaxed me maternally.

I didn't mind that. In fact she must have known that that was exactly what I needed at the time. I was almost bending over her. She pulled me a little more and put her lips on mine.

This was something new for her. During those earlier days it was I who made the first move. I had to do something to arouse her first. I used to fear at times that she never had an orgasm. But she put my doubts at rest. She said she used to affect passivity in order to excite and tease me.

Those divine dancers with their appealing thirsty lips carved in medieval temples arouse extraordinary aesthetic bliss in the spectator. But when one has a similar experience in real life all one sees is darkness. Lust, love, and darkness are perhaps the peaks of that excitement that dances like a deer in one's nerves and brain.

Bindo lay relaxed and naked before me. She had peeled off all her clothes. Bindo's naked body is nearly flawless. It makes one greedy. When an ordinary woman disrobes herself, it seems as if she is merely baring her body. I have never had this feeling with Bindo. When she slips out of her clothes, I feel as if she is about to immerse herself in a pool.

I noticed there was no decline in her body except that her breasts were a little fuller. The moment I touched them, they fluttered a bit. She opened her eyes and shut them again fast. She had some modesty left in them still. She smiled without opening her eyes. Then she raised herself a little and touched my chest with her cheek.

"This shirt," she whispered. "Never mind, you'll catch cold."

"No, I won't," I said and began to take off my shirt.

"Wait a second then. Let me get up first."

She got up and went into the other room. When she came back she had those two heaters in her hands.

To see a woman walking about inside a room in the nude is an experience in itself. The entire woman is alive. Every limb has its own natural form and there is a mysterious contrast between the body above the waist and that below the waist which breaks the monotony and the woman becomes extraordinarily delightful to look at. A woman standing in the nude is capable of destroying empires. The will-power of a man melts down like a pillar of wax and the body of the woman on seeing this blossoms all the more.

The warmth of the heaters came straight to our naked bodies. The blue light of the light bulb and the red heat of the heater fell on the back and thighs of Bindo like two little flags as she sat on the bed clinging to me. She squeezed me even more as I caressed her back. She was trying to merge her body into mine. I had never seen Bindo so excited. In fact it embarrassed me a little to see her like that. But whatever she was doing was quite natural. I have always held that a woman should give of herself without any reservation whatsoever. It is not always possible for most women to do that. At least Bindo had never done that before. She always held herself back. It was only when she couldn't that she used to ask me to kiss her on the breasts. And when I ran my tongue from her shoulders to her breasts and kissed them she was ecstatic and became one with my body.

This time Bindo didn't have to ask me. I remembered. I was doing my best to guide her gently to the beach so that I could toss her to the waves of the ocean. Her eyes were closed in ecstasy.

There is only one moment when a woman really loves her man, when she depends on him, when he controls her destiny. Bindo had accepted me as her master. Was it I taking revenge or was it she? I was pulled up short by this question.

"Where have you gone?" she asked, her face hidden from me.

"Nowhere. Get me a cigarette, will you?"

I could have easily got up myself for the cigarette. But it gave me some satisfaction to order her about like a master. She got up and brought me the pack of cigarettes. When I took one out she promptly lit it for me. I noticed in the glow of the light that her face was red. Was it a blush, was it the light, or was it anger?

She sat down on my hand where it lay on the quilt. The pressure of her buttocks pleased me. I did not remove my hand from under her.

"You have gained weight, it seems."

"Hmm."

"You look bigger than before."

And she was. Although one wouldn't notice it unless one came too close.

She looked at me so as to say, "So what!" And then she reclined on me with all her weight.

This tickled me as well as quickened the flow of blood in my veins.

Now she started kissing me passionately while I just lay there without any desire. Suddenly she squeezed my earlobe rather hard and hurt me.

"Why are you doing this?" I said irritably.

"To see whether you are awake or asleep," she said with a burst of laughter. "It doesn't look like you are awake. It seems only I am." Then she looked askance at me.

She was wrong. If I had become slack it was because I had forced myself to. And she knew that. In her own way she was challenging me again. I was amused by her womanly wiles. She had captured my body and was examining me victoriously. In her effort to dupe me she is deceiving herself, I thought.

"Promise," she said coquettishly like a little girl, "that you won't desert me again."

It was ridiculous that the woman at whose feet I had fallen and begged her forgiveness should be seeking this assurance from me. Perhaps she wanted to arouse the male in me and the female in herself in order to bring about the normal sportiveness that is there between an ordinary couple. But can we ever be an ordinary couple? For Bindo life is like a robe. But can I ever be like her? Can I ever be what I am not?

"Well, won't you answer me?" she said as she looked at me doubtfully. "Never mind. Maybe I shouldn't have even raised that issue."

I wondered whether she had said that sulkily. I didn't want her to sulk, for then I would have to appease her. I didn't want to have to appease her because that would mean I still valued her.

"You've changed a lot, you know," she said as she placed a soft pillow between her breasts. "Now you don't fly into rage, nor do you show any disgust. You even talk less. You *have* changed."

I should have retorted, "It's all thanks to you." It was true that compared to the past I was more self-controlled. But was it self-control that I had desired after all? One makes all sorts of sacrifices for something but the thing one actually achieves in the end after having lost everything in exchange is not what one really wanted.

I knew she hadn't made that remark approvingly. In fact she seemed quite weary of me by now. She was feeling bored and suffocated. Earlier our quarrels were always open, which meant some link in spite of pleasantness. It also was more fun.

She made another effort. She clung to me in order to arouse me. Her body was warm, which I liked.

Years ago, before I knew Bindo, I once had an affair with an older woman. She had reached me via several other men. That was my first time with a woman. The body of one's first woman, even if she is loose and worn out, leaves behind some pleasurable memories. I never loved her, nor did she have any delusions about our affair. Whenever she raised her lips to mine as she lay under me, I was reminded of the same scene: a bitch licking its mate with grateful delight. One day that same woman while kissing me in that way said to me, "You will make a wonderful lover." So it wasn't a good girl who had initiated me but a dirty old woman. It was she who made me realize that one needs love too.

I felt pity for that woman. I still do. She had accepted to begin with that she wasn't worthy of me. She never gave herself any airs. She could have if she had wanted to. But perhaps she knew from her own experience the complicated consequences of vanity. Our relationship was quite clear. There was not a touch of guilt anywhere.

But with Bindo it was different. She had

always been very demanding. At that moment more than ever.

I ran my hand over her unsmooth hips and closed her eyes with my fingers. Instead of love there was fear in those eyes. She seemed to struggle with that fear for a few minutes and then she opened her eyes again and started staring at me.

"You seem to have gone into a trance," she said haltingly with dry lips. She had her hand on my thigh. Her accusation was quite correct. A woman is the first to know when a man is without desire.

"Not at all!" I said. I had myself been trying to arouse myself but in vain. "Get me a glass of water."

As she went out to get water I switched off the light. It could have been because of the light. And because of the suddenness of the whole thing.

As she came back with water, she said, "Why did you turn the light off? I can't see a thing."

Does she have to see my unmanliness? Won't she let me mask it as my self-control?

I felt a little better after the water. I felt less afraid. It hasn't happened before and it won't today. I recalled the words of that older woman: You'll make a wonderful lover! Bindo sat with her breasts against my back. I liked that pressure of her full breasts and wanted her to keep it there. Then I straightened the quilt and covered myself and her properly with it.

I felt my blood flowing like a swarm of ants through my entire body. My ears began to tingle and my muscles were rippling again. I held her tightly to myself.

The woman whose pride I want to break, the woman who has always put me down is now in my hands. In a few minutes I will crush her, smash her to pieces, destroy that cherished soul of hers. Will she be able to bear my gaze after that in the light?

The impulse to see her in the light became imperative. I had turned off the light; I put out my hand and turned it on again. Bindo was taken aback. She couldn't understand why I had done that. I had thought I'd see fear on her face. My guess was correct. She looked terrified. Her body seemed stiff. The fear of giving of oneself distorts one's body, disfigures one's mouth, and perverts one's personality. The first time I had seen Bindo in that way was quite natural. At that time her fear was the fear of a school girl. But now it was the fear of a gambler.

Had Bindo been able to see through me she would have seen more wrinkles in my personality than in her own. But she had been interrupted in the last moment of her orgasm and her eyes had narrowed to a point of total unawareness.

Man alone brings a woman out of unawareness and takes her into another world of unawareness. By entering her he proves himself and reassures her at the same time.

She was breathing heavily like a patient of bronchitis. I had to end her agony. A little more force and that net would break through which light as well as darkness seeps into one's inside.

She closed her eyes once again. She was vibrating, her body linked with mine. Because of our vigorous movements the quilt had slipped off the bed.

But I hadn't thought I'd be over so soon. She still held on to me tightly. It seemed I had spilled over prematurely because I had been starving for a long time. It had happened a couple of times before that also. But I hadn't felt humiliated then. That day, however, after I had almost conquered her, I shouldn't have been defeated so near the end.

I expected she would scorn me and I wouldn't

be able to face her. So I started thinking of self-justifications. But nothing of the sort happened. Bindo looked at me fondly. There was no grievance in her glance. Is she just consoling me? Or is this all she had expected? I was alarmed. Had she let me make love to her only for form's sake? Without any expectation of pleasure for herself?

Perhaps that was the truth, for after that Bindo didn't make another move. She threw me a towel. She perhaps knew I wouldn't like to get up and go to the bathroom.

"There is hot water," she informed me.

Did she really want to go back to sleep? I couldn't believe it. Maybe she was being sarcastic again. I began to feel nervous. I couldn't make out how she could be so cool. She was about to put on her clothes.

"Don't," I said.

"Why?"

"Because."

She looked at me so as to say, "Do you want to go on for the rest of the night?" I wanted to say yes.

"Pull the quilt over," I said.

She pulled the quilt over quietly and I covered her and myself up carefully. She is being deceitful again. She has been deceitful all evening. She wanted to prove that I was no good even in bed. Was I being unfair to her?

It didn't take me too long to arouse myself. I was getting ready for a violent bout. I gave her a good shove where she lay next to me. Her eyes came open. She was only pretending to be sleepy, I told myself. She didn't say yes or no but just lay there next to me inertly. Frigid and lifeless! A while ago I was lifeless, now she was. I was about to utter something but she put her hand on my mouth so as to suggest, "Don't spoil the fun by saying anything."

She knows I'll take much longer the second time. And she doesn't like that. She can't brook the idea that I should emerge victorious. She doesn't want to see me victorious because she doesn't want to accept I can be.

She was awake now because of my roughness. She remonstrated in a rapt tone, "Won't you save something for tomorrow or must you spend yourself totally tonight?"

I was wearing her out. I was also wearing myself out. The more angry I became the more aggressive I grew. Against whom was this revenge? Against her or myself or against my destiny?

For me it was a revenge. For her perhaps it was nothing. She was no longer inert. She was reciprocating quite vigorously in fact. In spite of the cold we were drenched in sweat.

In one's most naked moments one wants to curse someone. It gives one pleasure. When one is with a woman one says all sorts of incoherent thing—swear words as well as some other strange meaningless sounds. The woman takes all these outbursts as part of love.

"You have gone limp," I said.

I thought she'd feel insulted but instead she smiled like a whore.

"I have changed again," she said as she pressed her hands against my back and pushed me into her. She was quite vigorous. There was no sign of any weariness in her.

When I finally came I felt extremely relieved. She lay there stretched out and exhausted.

"I don't want to get up," she said.

But I had to. I did, cleaned myself, and lit a cigarette. I felt light and my eyes were full of blissful sleep. But it wasn't bliss. It was a mere mirage. It would cause me a lot of pain, many regrets, and everlasting agony.

Next morning on waking up I found I was all alone in bed. It was quarter past eight. I got up in a great hurry. To wake up in another person's house, in another person's bed, is like being born again. I felt I had survived a shipwreck and swum on a plank to some island where slowly I was regaining my consciousness now. The more I remembered everything, the more panicky I was.

I put on my clothes as fast as I could and sat down on that sofa chair. I didn't dare to go into the other room. How will I face the servant? I was afraid but apparently Bindo wasn't, for I heard her ordering him about in the other room.

She came in with tea. She looked absolutely natural. I didn't see any trace of uneasiness on her face. But I couldn't look her in the eye.

"Here is some tea for you, breakfast will be along presently," she said and snuggled up to me.

My own body seemed odd to me. Even though Bindo had rearranged everything nicely, everything seemed repulsive to me.

Somehow I gulped the tea and went into the bathroom. When I came out, she had gone into the kitchen.

I stepped out of that room stealthily, cast a casual glance over things in the other room. My picture still perched quite possessively on the shelf. She didn't know that one is so different from one's image that no photograph can ever be true to one.

After I had crossed the street I started walking as fast as I could. I would have loved to run desperately and had there been an ocean nearby I'd have run straight into it.

6

Tormented by shame and defeat I reached home and collapsed on my bed. No sooner had I covered my face with the newspaper than the phone rang. I ordered the servant not to pick it up. I knew it was Bindo. The phone rang for quite some time. Then it stopped awhile and started ringing again.

I should leave this city and run away to some other place where I will never run into Bindo. But this is impossible. I can't go away from here. Then she should. Why had she come back in the first place?

I felt I had lost the last shred of self-respect. She had crushed me like a bat. I was good for nothing; I wasn't good even for her.

I hadn't slept much the previous night. So with my face covered by the newspaper I fell asleep. I was dimly aware of being disturbed a couple of times but I didn't wake up. When I finally did it was about noon. I shaved and went in for a shower.

I didn't know what to do or where to hide myself. Bindo was not Bindo but my veritable doom. I didn't know how to save myself from that doom. The previous night came back to me in spite of all my efforts to keep it out of my mind.

I had a hurried meal and left my place quietly. At Vijay Square I stretched myself on the green grass. That place had never been one of my haunts. There were a number of people lolling about on the grass. A few of them were enjoying the sun during office time while the rest were just bums. Nobody would recognize me there or call me by my name. Nobody would bother me with love. Nobody would humiliate me. I was one of the hundreds of people passing the time of the day on the grass. I took off my jacket and covered my face with it. I didn't want anyone to see my face. I wanted to lie there completely incognito. My pack of cigarettes lay on my chest.

At a short distance from me a few people were playing cards.

I could hear a hawker selling oranges. I will come here and get lost every day. This is the right place for me. Home is bunk. Bindo is bunk. Whatever I have known and experienced so far is bunk.

Lying there like that I again dozed off. When I opened my eyes again it was 3.30 p.m. My head was slightly heavy, I felt like a cup of tea. Just as I got up I saw a woman advancing toward me from some distance. She had on a green sweater and an untamed bearing. I was alarmed. But thank God as she came closer I noticed it wasn't Bindo.

I took a cup of tea at one of the little stalls nearby and headed toward the British Council library. I whiled away some time in the art exhibitions in the basement before walking up to the library.

The spotlessly clean library was almost empty except for a couple of absorbed readers. I walked over to a corner and started turning over the newspapers. When I got bored with the political news I picked up a popular magazine. But that did not hold my interest for too long. There should have been some whodunit fiction here, I muttered to myself. Whodunit? Bindo or I? Who is the culprit? Is Bindo the same woman I have known or some other woman whom I never got to know? Can I claim even now that I know her? But I don't need to know her, I told myself. I picked up a medical journal. Instead of trying to know oneself or others it is better to try to learn about diseases. But that journal had nothing to offer a layman. It was a research journal.

For over an hour I tried to calm myself in there. It was getting close to six and outside it was completely dark now. The library looked busier because of the last-minute borrowers and returners.

I got up to go. As I was walking to the door, I felt a soft tap on my back. I turned and found it was Bindo.

"You? Here?" I was astonished.

"I was sitting over there."

"Since when?"

"Oh, for the last one hour or so."

"How did you know?" I was annoyed.

"I did!"

As we walked down the stairs, she said, "I looked for you at several places before coming here."

She slipped her arm into mine. When we were in the light I noticed she looked prettier and happier than ever. She had kajal in her eyes and a bindi on her forehead.

As we came out of the building I looked at her inquisitively.

"Let us go to the movies," she said flirtatiously.

When I didn't react she became quiet. But she held on to my arm and walked very close to me. My own arm dangled like a dead snake.

"Why did you slip away like that?" she complained.

After a pause she went on, "Why didn't you pick up the phone?"

Either she is an idiot or she is just pretending to be one. I didn't dare even to look straight at her.

"Are you mad at me?" she asked as she snuggled even closer.

People passing by stared at us. Perhaps they envied us our blissful togetherness. Nobody would even suspect the truth. If Bindo didn't who else would?

"Let us walk over to that spot. On the grass."

She was pointing toward the canal.

"The grass is wet. Dew," I said faintly.

"So what?"

So I allowed myself to be dragged to the canal. As I was looking for a dry spot, she spread her handkerchief and said, "Here! Your pants won't be spoiled."

All around us in the dim light there were other couples strolling and sitting. Everybody seemed oblivious of others.

"What a lovely spot! Why didn't you ever bring me here?" she complained. Then she went on, "Maybe it is a recent addition."

A couple passed by us and left clouds of perfume behind.

"Aren't there flowers for sale somewhere nearby?" she asked as she rested her head on my shoulder. I caressed her hair dutifully.

"Let us go over there," she said abruptly as she got up and pointed to a totally unlit spot.

I walked along with her like an automaton to that spot. I sat down while she put her forehead on my lap and stretched herself on the grass unmindful of the dew. The darkness was gathering in my inside like phlegm. It seemed there was no way out. Is there really no way out?

"Do you have no interest in me at all?" she said calmly as she lay there.

I get terribly upset by this simple question. Even in those days she often raised it. And in order to convince her of my interest I had to do all sorts of things I didn't believe in. So I decided to turn a deaf ear to her now.

She repeated her question. And when I again pretended I hadn't heard her she sat up. She gazed at me. I saw a glow on her face similar to the ones she had just before an outburst. So there we were again. Or was I wrong.

I got up.

"Where will you go?" I asked.

She gave me a puzzled look.

"Don't you want to go home?" I asked in a low voice.

"So soon?" she said as she looked askance at me. "Maybe you are in a hurry," she added sizing me up. "Well, in that case, I can walk home by myself," she said sourly.

She unhooked her arm. She is stubborn! Let her go to hell!

She paused for a moment and turned toward the direction of her place.

"Wait a moment," I said.

I was in darkness. She stopped. I walked over to her and said, "I'll walk you home."

After we had walked some distance, I stopped and sat down on a sort of rock. She sat down beside me, close.

"You look exhausted," she said and clung to me like ivy.

I couldn't see her and she couldn't see me. With my face averted from her, in the dark, clutching at my chest with my left hand, I sobbed silently.